D1297182

MOON & STARS

WHISKEY RIVER WEST

KELLY MOORE

Edited by KERRY GENOVA

Illustrated by DARK WATER COVERS

Photography by PAUL HENRY SERRES

Kelly Moore

MOON & STARS - PART 2

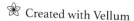

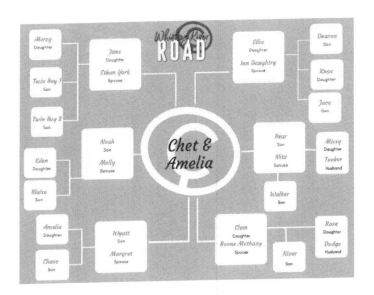

Whiskey River ROAD

Chet & Amelia

Mercy
Daughter

Twin Boy 1
Son

Twin Boy 2
Son

Jane
Daughter
Ethan York
Spouse

Eden
Daughter

Blaise
Son

Noah
Son
Molly
Spouse

Amelia
Daughter

Chase
Son

Wyatt
Son
Margret
Spouse

Ellie
Daughter
Jan Daughtry
Spouse

Deacon
Son

Knox
Daughter

Jace
Son

Bear
Son
Nita
Spouse

Missy
Daughter
Tucker
Husband

Walker
Son

Clem
Daughter
Boone Metheny
Spouse

River
Son

Rose
Daughter
Dodge
Husband

METHANY BRAND

I'd gather the sun, the moon, and the stars for the ones I love.

CHAPTER ONE
RIVER

"I'm done with you!" I catch the tail end of my shirt in the hood when I slam it shut. "Son of a..." It rips off, leaving a plaid strip of material hanging when I yank it out. "I've been so loyal to you for years, not ditching your sorry ass in the junkyard, and this is how you repay me!" I kick the tire with the toe of my boot in my rant, looking like an idiot, scolding my truck.

"Where's my phone?" I pat the pockets of my jeans, searching for it. I bolt to the driver's side, slinging open the door, and it nearly falls to the dirt. Looking on the dash and in the center console, I don't see it. "Where the hell are you?" Sliding my hand between the seat and the console, I feel it but can't reach it. Taking a step back, with my hands glued to my hips, tilting my head toward the sun, I close my eyes and take a deep breath, desperate to calm down. It doesn't help. "The woman I want more than anything is halfway around the world by now!" Why couldn't I find the words I wanted to say instead of stammering like a fool?

Leaning over the seat, I weasel my hand in the crevice, stretching my fingers as far as I can. "Come on." I grit my teeth for control. "Got it!" I yell, grasping it between two fingers. The phone flies out of my hand when I sit up quickly, whipping around to call Chase for help. It crashes on the asphalt, shattering the screen. "No, no, no!" I roar, frantically picking it up. "Please work," I grovel, then growl when I tap on the screen, and it goes black. "Hell's bells! Can't anything go in my favor?" Tossing it on the road, I stomp on it with the heel of my boot, then jump when I hear a horn honk.

"Whatcha doing there, cowboy?" Knox pulls up next to me.

Zipping to the passenger side, I lift the handle. "Unlock the door. I need a ride," I shout through the closed window. She presses the button, unlocking it. "I need to find Greer." I point out the windshield.

"What's got you all riled up like a wet owl?" she

says, staring at me with a firm grip planted on the steering wheel.

"I messed things up with Greer, and I've got to fix it!" My hands fly in the air with my palms facing one another as if I'm preaching.

"What did you do?" Her southern drawl is exaggerated, grating under my skin.

"Just drive!" I holler, pointing again at the road.

She shoves the car in park and angles toward me, crossing her arms over her chest. "I ain't going anywhere until you calm the hell down and tell me what happened."

I rock back and forth with my fingertips pressed against my eyelids. "She thinks I was willing to sacrifice her for my family. Her father told her if she'd go back to work for him and stay away from me, he'd leave me alone, but she didn't believe him."

"Did you tell her absolutely, under no circumstance, would she work for him again?" Her voice raises.

"In my mind, I was trying to figure out a way to protect her."

"Let me guess." She turns, facing the steering wheel. "You didn't get the words out fast enough to tell her you love her, and you'd never let that happen," she snorts.

"She didn't give me a chance. She was all fire mad and wouldn't quit talking long enough to let me finish my thoughts. And then"—I inhale sharply—"my truck wouldn't start, so I couldn't go after her."

"Did you at least tell her you're in love with her?" My annoyance grows when she rolls her eyes at me.

"She didn't give me a chance!" I spat in frustration.

"You mean to tell me you've been paddling up her coochie creek, and you haven't told her you love her yet?" She shoves the car into drive, laughing at me.

I'm caught between a laugh and a snarl. "Just drive already!"

"Men are such dumbasses." She's shaking her head.

"Look. I'm not good at this sort of thing. Love has brought me nothing but trouble, so do you think I wanted to hop on the bandwagon? I believe in love, but I sure wasn't looking for it, nor did I want it. Greer took me by surprise and way faster than I ever thought possible. I want to be the person she cuddles with at four a.m. and gives sleepy kisses to. I didn't want to fall in love, not at all, but at some point, it wasn't a choice anymore. She blew me out of the water when she smiled at me, saying my name."

She reaches over, popping me in the back of the head. "Why didn't you say those things to her? If you had, we wouldn't be chasing her down right now."

My head droops, and my shoulders sag. "I don't know." I exhale loudly.

The car jerks forward with her tapping on the pedal. "Where do you think she went?"

"I'm guessing her aunt's house where she's been staying."

"Alright, we'll start there. Once we find her, you need to convince her to move in with us. It's the only way you can protect her from her horrible father. You and I are lucky we had parents who loved us, no matter what. They'd never threaten our lives. Greer must be beside herself. Can you imagine your father being so cruel?" She glances in my direction, taking her focus off the road for a few seconds. "No wonder she ran. She doesn't know what unconditional love feels like, and you not being able to express it has her not knowing where to turn."

"You're right. I'll make sure to fix it with her. Can I use your phone? I need to call Chase and put him on high alert from Alden."

She hands it to me. I get ahold of him, letting

him know Alden's ultimatum to Greer and that if she happens to show up, to not let her go.

"Her Bronco is here," I state as Knox pulls into the driveway of Greer's aunt's house. I jump out, sprinting before she has it in park. My knuckles rap hard on the door. "Greer!" I yell. "I'm sorry! Please let me in!" I knock several more times.

Mrs. Alden opens the door. "I'm afraid you've missed her," she says, with her dark brows furrowing together.

"But her car is here." I twist my body in its direction.

"My sister took her to the airport about fifteen minutes ago."

I brace a hand on the door. "Did she tell you where she's going?"

Her terse gaze skims from my boots to my eyes. "She said she'd figure it out once she got there. Greer needed to leave. In fact"—she juts her chin in the air —"I encouraged it with the way things are with her father. You were the icing on the cake for her. I must say, I was quite surprised. It was only a few hours ago she was singing your praises, telling me how much she loved you."

"Please, if you know anything about where she went, I have to find her," I plead.

She folds her arms over her chest. "I haven't done a very good job in protecting my daughter up until now. I'll be keeping her whereabouts to myself when I know where she is."

I scratch the side of my face. "I love her, and I need to tell her."

"Seems to me if you'd have said those words to her face, she'd be here."

I tip the brim of my Stetson and run back to the car, slamming the door. "She left for the airport fifteen minutes or so ago."

Knox spins her tires, backing out, and I have to hold on for dear life when she does an about-face on a dime. "Dang woman," I say, buckling my seat belt. "You drive this thing like you're riding a horse."

"Where do you think I learned to operate a car?" She laughs, going Mach nine out onto the road. "Did she say where she was going?"

"She claims she doesn't know, but even if she did, she wouldn't tell me. Her mother chooses now to be loyal to her daughter of all times."

"We'll find her." She clasps my shoulder.

"I don't blame her for running. I did the same thing when things got too hard. Her heart's broken by me, and her father is the devil. What choice did she have?"

"We all have choices, River. You moving away from Salt Lick was a good one. This is just a small hitch in your giddy-up. You're going to find a way to defeat Alden and get the girl."

"You make it sound like a fairy tale. I'm not good at happy endings."

"Then we're going to change the ending of your story." She smiles broadly. "I'll drop you off out front and wait for you," she says, pulling over into the departure lane.

Kicking the door open, I run to security, trying to convince them to let me in to find her. "You'll have to buy a ticket to get to the gates," the man says firmly.

As I turn to leave, I see Greer pulling her luggage by the handle behind her, walking fast. "Greer!" I yell, waving my arms like a maniac. She doesn't look in my direction. After calling her name again, I see an earbud lodged in her ear. "Please, she's right there," I plead to the man, pointing at her.

"You need a ticket." His voice is stern as he glares at me for holding up his line.

I watch her enter the gate and scan her boarding pass, then disappear onto the walkway of the airplane. "Can you at least tell me where the plane is headed?" I beg.

"You'll have to check over there." He motions in the direction with a tilt of his head.

I scan the large digital board, looking for the gate number. "Cincinnati? Why would she go there?" I'm baffled, wondering if she has family in Ohio she never mentioned. Her mother isn't going to tell me. Perhaps it's a connecting flight. Slowly, I meander outside and find where Knox has been waiting.

"Did you find her?" she asks, peering over my shoulder through the window of the car.

"I did, but she didn't hear me, and they wouldn't let me through the gate without a ticket. She was on a plane to Ohio before I could purchase one."

"Ohio? What the heck is she going to Ohio for?"

"I don't know. It could be a connecting flight to anywhere." I slam the door, banging my forehead on the dash. "It's too late. I've lost her."

"Don't think that way. She probably just needed to get away to clear her mind." She rubs my back. "She'll remember how much she loves you and come back home."

"I hope you're right, but if I had someone threatening the lives of the people I loved, and if I thought it was the only way to keep them safe, I'd stay away too. She thinks she's doing the right thing."

"But didn't you say she said the agreement was if

she went back to work for him, he'd leave you alone? Her running away isn't working for him."

"Then she left because she hates me." I sigh.

"She doesn't hate you, but that means your life is in danger." She slams on the gas pedal. "Alden can't get his hands on Granger, so you're going to be his target."

"I'm going to stop him once and for all." I grind my teeth.

"You talking about killing him?" She raises a brow.

"I'm going to cut him off at the knees. And by knees, I mean Lance. He's the one that will come after me, not Alden himself."

"What are you going to do?"

"I'll set myself as bait, and he'll take it. Chase and Blaise can help me set him up."

"The sheriff ain't going to arrest him."

"I'll have it on video. He'll have no choice, and I'm betting his father will turn against his son if he fails so that he won't look bad."

"Please don't go and get yourself killed. I'm kinda liking it here," she teases, trying to lighten the situation.

"I don't plan on going anywhere. Whiskey River

West is our home, and I will protect it and the people living there."

She drives like crazy back to the ranch. "We need to have a family meeting," I snarl into the radio I grabbed, marching into the house. Mercy and Walker are in the kitchen. Within five minutes, Chase and Blaise storm in the back door. They all gather around the table, taking a seat.

"I'm going to set a plan in motion to take down Alden before he has a chance to follow through on his threats. You and Blaise"—I point to Chase—"are going to help me set up Lance. Once he's out of the picture, Alden will back down, not wanting to hurt the precious reputation he thinks he has with the people in this town."

"Where's Greer?" Mercy asks.

"She's gone." I swallow my words hard, not wanting to believe it. "So, she's safe from him."

"Gone. Like where?" she asks.

Knox grits her teeth and shakes her head at Mercy to get her to let it go.

"It's not important, only that she's safe." I talk over her. "What is important is that we stick to a plan. Mercy and Knox will stay on the property with men guarding them and the house. Walker, I want you to make sure no one comes on this land unless they've been cleared by you."

"I want to help." Mercy rises.

"I appreciate it, but it's too risky. You can help me by staying put until it's all over."

CHAPTER TWO
GREER

"Are you alright, ma'am?" The flight attendant hands me a small package of tissues.

Adjusting my sunglasses closer to my face, I wipe away a tear. "I'm fine, thank you." I sniff, taking them from her. I'm thankful the flight wasn't full, and I was able to get a window seat in a row by myself.

I had no idea where I was going when my aunt dropped me off at the airport. All I knew was that I needed to get away. From my father... from River... from my life in general. Cincinnati was the first flight leaving Missoula, so I bought a ticket.

I don't know what I was thinking. If I were in River's shoes, my first priority would be my son. Not some messed-up substitute school teacher that I'd barely just met with a treacherous father who wants nothing more than to destroy the life he's trying to build for his family. I wouldn't want me either. But what I'd give to be loved by him and his family. What would it feel like to have a father fly thousands of miles just to help me? I blow my nose, determined not to cry anymore.

If River loved me, not that he ever told me such, he would've come after me instead of letting me drive away. I'm such a stupid woman. I fail miserably at my attempt to not shed any more tears.

"Can I get you anything?" The poor flight attendant must think me pathetic.

"Black coffee, please." I wipe my nose and pull up the small window blind so I can see the landscape as we fly over it.

"Anything else?" Her eyes and tone are gracious.

"No. Thank you for your kindness." I take the cup in both hands, holding it under my nose. Blowing on it to cool it down, I reach for the magazine in the back of the seat in front of me when I see the name of a state in bold, bright letters. Visit Kentucky. Home of the Kentucky Derby, and The Bluegrass State, is what the headline says. "Salt Lick," I whisper. I can't flip the pages fast enough to look at the map in the middle. Calculating quickly, it's about a two-hour drive from where I land if I can't catch another flight.

Closing my eyes, I envision what it would be like to meet all of River's family. To know where he comes from... to know how it feels to be part of it. They've built a good, loyal, protective son. I can't fault him for pushing me away. My father created bullies and a man full of hate. Lance doesn't even know why he's so hateful, only that my father groomed him to be that way. And a daughter who didn't have any idea what love was until River crashed into my heart. A hard sob escapes thinking about him and the moments we've spent in each other's arms. I press my lips together, still feeling his kiss and the taste of him.

Opening my eyes, I rip out the map, shoving it into my carry-on bag. Even if I can't ever have him again, I want to know what it would feel like to be part of his family. My father may take everything else away from me, but he can't have this. I sniff my last tear, straightening my spine. "Salt Lick, here I come."

I settle into my seat, enjoying the rest of the flight as I watch an old movie on my phone while it charges. As soon as we land, I turn the Wi-Fi on to see if I have any messages. Holding my breath, I wait and watch. Nothing. My shoulders sag. "He didn't even try to call me," I whisper and shrug my carry-on over my shoulder. My dress swishes between my boots as I make my way to see when the next flight to Kentucky leaves.

"May I help you?" the lady behind the counter, dressed in a crisp white button-down shirt and navy pants, asks with a polite smile.

"When is the next flight to…" I pull out the map, unfolding it. "To Lexington, Kentucky." It's the closest city to Salt Lick.

She taps the keys on her computer. "The next flight out isn't until tomorrow morning. I'll check other airlines for you," she says, scanning the screen. "Nothing any sooner."

"Thank you for looking." I exit to the car rental area.

After the car is inspected, the agent hands me the keys to a sporty red convertible Mustang. I could've chosen an SUV, but I want to feel Kentucky on my skin. Tossing my bags in the back seat, I get behind the wheel and set my GPS to the city of Salt Lick.

My drive takes me by the Kentucky Derby, where smaller races are currently being held. I'd love to see the Derby in its grand fair with ladies dressed in their fancy hats and the crowds cheering for the horses. I bet River has been here at least a dozen times.

The bluegrass of Kentucky is no exaggeration. It's utterly stunning but flatter than Montana. It has rolling hills and a few buttes, but nothing compared to the mountains surrounding Missoula.

The terrain changes as I drive out of the city to wide open pasture lands crisscrossed with cattle. Some small ranches, others covering vast acres of property. There are tall trees with heavy leaves and winding creeks mingled in them. Round bales of hay are speckled in the fields. The air smells like the sweet hay has just been cut. Ranch-style houses seem to be a common theme, nestled among grain silos, large red barns, and acres of vegetables, with greenhouses in the backdrop. There are fields of yellow flowers and seedy heads of wheat for miles on end. There's a farmer climbing out of his tractor, wearing a flannel shirt and an old pair of work boots. He waves as I drive by. Another house has a tire swing hanging from a giant oak tree, with children running and playing. It's peaceful and heavenly at the same time.

My GPS directs me to a dirt road. "This can't be it." I pull over, shielding my eyes from the sun.

"Whiskey River Road," I read the small green street sign. Opening my door, I walk to the fence lined with barbed wire, watching the livestock graze. How many times has River worked this pasture, I wonder to myself? In the distance, there's a shirtless man splitting wood on an old tree stump. He stops, wipes his brow, and jerks his head in my direction when he sees me. He hops on an ATV and drives toward me. I stumble over a root, trying to get back to the Mustang and end up with my feet in the air and my dress around my waist.

"Are you lost?" a deep southern voice asks after the sound of the motor turns off.

I tug my dress over my bum before I take his outstretched hand, garnering the feel of pink on my cheeks. "I'm sorry. I was just admiring your land and cattle." I brush the clay off my knees,

He chuckles, and it reminds me of River's laugh. "Ain't my land. Wish it was. My family owns this property."

"Whiskey River." I point to the sign.

"Yes, ma'am. It's all owned by the Calhoun family."

I can't help but stare at his sweaty bare chest. He's a little taller than River but has just as big of guns on his arms. I'd say he was closer to Chase's age than River's.

He grins when he notices my stare. "Sorry, I was cutting wood." He folds his arms over his bare chest. "I'm Deacon Daughtry. Do you have a name?"

Daughtry. Not Calhoun. "Do you work for the Calhouns?" I ask.

"My last name may be Daughtry, but I'm as Calhoun as they come. My mother's father, Chet Calhoun, owned every single blade of this property," he says with pride.

"I'm Greer." I hold out my hand.

"It's nice to meet you, Greer, from..." his voice trails off, waiting for a response.

"I'm just passing through. I've never been to Kentucky." I avoid answering that I'm from Montana. It might make him a little suspicious.

"We don't get too many pretty visitors like you on our land. Would you like to join me for a glass of lemonade?"

"Oh, I'm... I've got to get on the road," I say, backing away toward the car. I get in, shutting the door. "Is there a town close by? I'd like to grab some lunch before I head out."

"Turn around. When you see the red barn on the right, take a left. Then you'll pass two dirt roads before you come to a stop sign, where you're gonna turn right. Then drive three miles as the crow flies, and you'll be in the center of town. There's a great cafe on the second block on Main St. My aunt Nita owns the place. Best darn pies you'll ever eat." He lifts his shoulder, wiping his forehead, and smiles.

"Thank you for your kindness," I say, turning the key.

He grips the door with both hands wide. "Sure I can't fix you a lemonade?"

"I appreciate it, but no, thank you."

He stands tall. "It was nice to meet you, Greer," he says. "Be careful of the potholes driving this fancy car."

"I will." I can't help but grin at him. I love his southern ways that are so much like River's.

I have no intention of going into town until the turn by the red barn. My car seems to have a mind of its own. If I'm going to hang around for a few days, I should find a hotel room. I'm sure they have one in town.

After the two dirt roads, my tires ease to a slow pace at the sign. Perched on top of the stop sign is a scarecrow. Someone has fastened its straw arm to a bar, with its hand pointing toward town. As I make the turn, I hear the sound of a large machine. A farmer is harvesting his field of corn.

Easing slowly into town, I find the cafe that Deacon suggested and park across the street in the only spot open. I briskly walk across the road when the light changes, and a bell jingles when I open the glass door to the cafe. The only open seating is at the bar-style countertop. The waitress lays a menu in front of me. Behind me is a table of older women, laughing up a storm at something.

"You must be new to town. I haven't seen you here before." A lady about the same age as the ones at the table, with long silvery-black hair braided to the side, says from behind the counter.

"I'm just passing through. This place came recommended by a friend." I smile a smile that matches hers.

"Well, welcome to Nita's Place." She giggles. "I'm Nita."

So she's Deacon's aunt. I wonder if she's River's mom. "You own the place and work here?"

"Not usually. Two staff members got married recently, and I'm covering their shifts." She points to the menu. "I'd highly recommend the patty melt. Best thing you'll ever put in your mouth beside my homemade pies."

"It's not the best thing I've ever put in my mouth," one lady at the table shouts, and they all roar in laughter.

"Keep your naughty thoughts to yourself," Nita scolds, then giggles, "until I can join you ladies."

"You must know everyone in town." I sip on the glass of water she fills.

"I've lived here a long time. I wasn't born here like most of the folks in these parts."

"Really? What brought you to Salt Lick, Kentucky?" She's piqued my curiosity.

"Pure luck. I'd gotten myself in a bit of trouble and was on the run," she says.

"You didn't rob a bank or anything?" I ask, leaning over the counter, whispering.

"She got her corn ground by my brother and never left town," a different woman says, snickering.

"Don't mind my sisters. They've always been dirty-minded." She shoos with her hand.

"Actually, they remind me of someone I know. It makes me feel right at home."

"Oh, sweet baby Jesus. You mean there's more like them in other parts of the world." She cackles.

I don't dare tell her Knox is from here. "There must be." I lift my glass to my lips.

"You're awfully pretty. Too bad my son Walker

doesn't live here anymore. I'd sure introduce the two of you."

So, not River's mom, but Walker's. I turn on the barstool to face the ladies at the table. She said they were her sisters. She must've meant in-laws because the attractive older lady sitting next to the window, with hints of brunette scattered in her hair, said brother. The minute she looks at me, I know it's River's mother. He has Boone's eyes, but his facial expressions mimic hers. I nearly drop my glass on the floor.

"You look as if you've seen a ghost," she says, handing a napkin to the woman beside her to give to me.

"I'm clumsy, that's all," I play it off.

The door chimes when it opens, and in walks two familiar faces. River's dad and son. I swivel in my chair and poke my face into the menu.

CHAPTER THREE

RIVER

"**D**o you have Greer's number stored on your phone?" I ask Mercy.

"Knox told me what happened. Why haven't you tried calling her before now?" She grips her cell phone to her chest.

"Are you going to lecture me too?" My dark-eyed gaze snaps to hers.

"From the sounds of it, you still need one. Perhaps I should call your mother. She's good at getting through to you." She toys with her phone.

"Fine! Go ahead, get it out of your system." I hang my head and let my hands fall loosely to my sides.

"First." She holds up one finger. "You have to admit to me out loud that you love her."

My mouth scrunches from side to side. "I love her," I mumble.

"That ain't good enough. I want you to say it loud enough that the cows in the west pasture can hear you." She spews her demands as thick as black smoke.

I inhale sharply and holler at the top of my lungs. "I love Greer Alden."

A satisfied smile races across her face, then she holds up two fingers. "Secondly, you'll get your head out of your ass and do something about it."

"Is there a third?" I ask sardonically.

She walks over to me, slapping the phone in the palm of my hand. "Marry her, and put us all out of your misery."

"I'm not ready..."

She pinches my lips between her fingers. "I didn't say marry her tomorrow, just please don't let her get away." She glares at me for a moment before she releases my lips from her grasp on them.

I hold the phone in the air. "If you haven't noticed, she's already gone."

"So? Lay the River Methany charm on and win her back." She lifts a single shoulder into a shrug.

"There is no such thing," I grumble, finding Greer's name in her phone.

"Now's the time to find it. And you're so wrong. If you weren't so in love with Paige, you would've seen all the girls throwing themselves at your feet. You stepped over all of them for her."

"Was I really that bad?" I ask, scratching the side of my head.

"Yes, you were."

"She's not exaggerating." Knox steps into the room, rinsing off her plate.

I wave between them. "You two have always tag-teamed up against me."

Knox dries her hands, walks over to me, and lightly smacks me on the cheek. "The difference is, this time, it's not against you, River. It's for you."

I step to the corner of the room, press Greer's name on the phone, and place it against my ear. It rings several times, then it's sent to voicemail.

"What time are we putting our plan into motion?" Chase says, bursting through the back door.

My words are caught in my throat. Instead of leaving a message, I hang up. "I'll be at the brewery at seven, running my mouth about Alden like we planned." I give the phone back to Mercy, and her scowl sets deep between her eyes.

"Good because the townspeople made their

voices heard. We have enough signatures on the list to overthrow the sheriff's position." He shoves several pieces of paper against my chest. "Looks like the entire town wants him out."

I shuffle through them. "You ain't kidding. How quickly can we act on this?"

"According to my father, it will take ten days to have the petition properly filed, then he can be removed by a town vote, and an acting sheriff has to be instated at the same time."

"Are you ready to be a sheriff again?" I ask, bracing my hand on his shoulder.

"I'm not only ready, I'm looking forward to it, even if it is only temporary," he says without one hitch in his voice.

It's good to see the old Chase come back to life. He's been through a lot, too, but he keeps it tucked inside. "Once Sheriff Grady gets served, it's going to be an all-out war with him and Alden."

"Then we'd better be prepared for the battle," he states, looking me squarely in the eyes.

"I found it," Blaise yells, coming down the stairs with a video camera in his hand.

"You still have that ancient monster?" Knox laughs at him.

"This was Grandpa Chet's. I'm never getting rid of it." He looks through the lens.

"That thing is so old, you can't play the tapes on anything," Mercy snickers.

"Please tell me you aren't planning on using it to record tonight?" Chase rubs his forehead.

"Gotcha." Blaise laughs. "I just wanted to see your face when you thought I'd be using it." He lays it on the table and tugs his cell phone from his pocket. "The trusty phone will work fine."

"Thank God. For a minute there, I thought he was serious." I pick up Grandpa's video camera. "We used to watch these every Friday night. My mom and dad wanted me to know our grandfather."

"I saw the videos. He was an ornery old bastard." Mercy grins.

"Yeah, but he had a sweet and loyal side too," Knox adds.

"This memory lane thing is all well and good, but I have work to do." Chase marches out of the house with the petition fisted in his hand.

"Who peed on his cornflakes?" Mercy asks.

"He's never been one for reminiscing." I totally get it.

"Have you spoken with Granger this morning?" Mercy asks, walking toward the living room.

"Yeah. He and my dad camped out in tents last night on the ranch. He's having a great time. They're meeting our mothers for an early dinner at the cafe."

"I bet they are spoiling him rotten." She laughs.

"He'll be difficult to deal with when he comes home. I'm missing him like crazy, but I'm happy he's getting to spend time with all of our families."

"I'm totally jealous," Knox says.

"You should go for a visit," I tell her.

"I will this winter when it gets cold here."

"Smart woman." I chuckle. "I'm going to go meet up with Walker to make sure he has the men lined up to watch the property. Chase put him in charge of it."

"Last time I saw him, he was in the corral, trying to tame that ornery horse again," Blaise says.

Sure enough, that's where I find him. I sit on the top rung of the fence and watch him. The horse, to my surprise, lowers his head, allowing Walker to put the bridle on him.

"Good boy," he says, scratching the horse behind the ear.

Copper barks, spooking the horse, and Walker calms him, moving slowly around the corral.

"Nice job." I clap.

"I told you I'd win." Walker smirks.

"You're the horse whisperer," I hoot.

"Honestly, I'm the one taking cues from him. Once he let me know what his fears were, we came to an agreement on how I'd broach him."

"Personally, I think you're crazy, but it worked. You've always had a way with animals, not just horses."

"You didn't come out here to watch me. What's up, cousin?"

"I wanted to see if you had the men securing the ranch."

"Yep. Everyone knows their job."

"The house will be double guarded tonight?"

"One man will be at the gate, one on the back step, and I'll be on the porch with my rifle. We will spread the other men all over the property line."

"Sounds like you have it handled."

"The only way a trespasser is leaving this property is in a body bag." He stops and looks at me. "Unless you want me to dig a hole where they fall and bury them."

"Nah, let's keep things on the up and up." That's exactly what my father would've done. I jump down. "Chase will carry the radio if you need anything."

Peeling out of my T-shirt, I give a hand to one of our men, who pulled up with a truck bed full of hay. We lift each one, hauling them under the pole barn. The bale scrapes against the truck bed as it's dragged off. Copper gets under my feet, nearly toppling me over.

"You're not helping," I groan, and he barks at me, waggling his tail. "Go chase a cow or something. I'll throw the ball with you later." I scratch under his chin.

I slam the tailgate shut when the last bale of hay is hauled out. Inside the barn, I slice open a bag of grain with the knife in a sheath attached to my hip. I pour it into a metal bucket, then fill the wooden troughs. When the stalls are cleaned and all the animals are fed, I sit on one of the bales, taking a break and wiping the sweat off my body with a towel. My biceps ache from lifting the hay. You'd think by now I'd be used to the work, but it's never-ending.

In the still of the moment, my mind wanders to Greer. *Where are you?* I wish I knew. I'd surely go after her. Once I have Lance in jail, and her father contained, I'm going to do everything in my power to find her. To make things right. She needs to know she owns my heart. What I'd give to hold her right now. To tell her I'm sorry. There should have been no hesitation on my part when it comes to her. She's not her father. She has an honest-to-goodness soul. To go against her family has to be hard. I hate to think she's somewhere feeling all alone. Shunned by a father and thinking the man she loves doesn't love her enough to fight for her.

"What are you doing out here? I thought you'd be getting ready to go?" Chase asks, sitting next to me. "You know we have men to do this work, right?"

"I do. But it feels good to get my hands dirty doing the hard work every now and then."

"Plus, it keeps your mind off Greer." He chuckles.

"I've messed up a lot of things in my life. I hope she isn't one of them."

"From where I sit, I think you've made a lot of good choices. You've got this place with men who respect you. A son who is going to grow up to be a good man because of you, despite his genetics. A family who has followed you to God's country to be by your side. And a woman who loves you. At least she did." He nudges me with his elbow.

"When you say it out loud, it all sounds pretty good, minus not knowing if Greer is coming back or not."

"Let's get through tonight, then you can concentrate on Greer."

I glance at my watch. "I'll head to the house and get a shower. We can meet on the porch in thirty minutes."

CHAPTER FOUR

GREER

My phone rings, drawing attention to me. I fumble to get it out of my purse before I can send the call to voicemail without even looking to see who it is.

"Grandpa and me had so much fun!" I hear the pure joy in Granger's voice.

"Have you decided what you'd like to order?" Nita drags the menu down to the table with one finger.

"I um... I'll have the patty melt like you suggested." I deepen my voice.

"Are you coming down with a cold or something?" She squints.

Picking up my water, I take a few sips. "My

throat's a little dry, that's all," I say softly. Before she walks away, I add, "And a piece of strawberry pie."

River's family is chatting among one another, but I get a feeling I'm being watched. Then I feel a small hand tap my shoulder. Squeezing my eyes shut, I try to act as if I didn't notice.

"Excuse me." He taps again.

"Granger. Get over here and leave the lady alone," his grandpa says.

"That ain't no lady. That's my daddy's girlfriend," his voice carries through the cafe.

I sit stock-still.

"Why would River's girlfriend be in Salt Lick?" I don't know the women's voices to tell who is asking.

A heavy chair scrapes the floor, and I bite my bottom lip.

"Greer?" Boone's tone is even.

I inhale and gradually turn to face him. "Hi," I say sheepishly, with a little wave.

He raises an eyebrow questioningly. "What are you doing here?"

"I told you it was her!" Granger runs into my arms for a hug.

River's mother gets to her feet and walks over to me. "I'm Clem, River's mother."

"It's so nice to meet you," I say, completely embarrassed.

"Is River here too?" she asks, looking around.

"No. It's just me." I wrinkle my nose.

"Did you miss me? Is that why you're here?" Granger lifts his head to look at me.

"I did miss you." I tweak his nose.

"How about you give her a little space?" Boone drags him off me.

Clem draws me in for a hug. "I don't care why you're here. I'm just so happy to meet the woman that has my son's heart."

I'm not sure she's right, but it feels good to be welcomed.

She lets go and turns toward the table. "This is River's family. At least the women. Ellie is my sister and Knox's mother." She smiles.

"Knox is a hoot." I giggle.

"Takes after her mother." Boone chuckles.

"Margret is married to my brother, Wyatt."

"Chase's parents," I say. "He is such a strong, gentle giant."

"It's so nice to meet you," Margret says sweetly.

"Molly is married to my second to the oldest brother, Noah."

"You'd be Blaise's parents. He's such a nice young

man." I get to my feet. "You must be Jane." I extend my hand. "I love Mercy so much. We've become good friends."

"She is a rare breed." She laughs.

"I'm Nita, married to Bear," she says from behind the counter.

"Walker is a gem. He's so good with horses."

"Please, join us." Boone pulls up a chair from a table that's just been vacated.

"Thank you," I say, taking a seat, and Granger plops down in the one next to me.

"Ain't she purty?" He props his elbows on the table with his chin resting on his hands, staring at me. "She was my girlfriend first, but I gave her up so my daddy could have her."

They all laugh.

"How did you meet River?" Jane asks.

"I'm a substitute teacher, and I was covering for Granger's teacher. Funny thing." I snicker. "I'd seen Mercy in the drop-off lane with Granger. She was having a bit of an issue..."

"That's when Aunt Mercy showed her middle finger to Sally's mom," Granger says, cutting me off. "She's not allowed to use the drop-off lane anymore."

"That sounds like Mercy." Jane smirks.

I ruffle Granger's hair and can't help but laugh. "She had to apologize to Sally's momma. Anyway, River had to pick him up from school that day until the issue could be worked out. I thought he and Mercy were married. It wasn't until a few days later, that she told me they were cousins."

"They act more like brother and sister. They've fought since they were little, but they always loved one another. Poor River couldn't get away with anything, especially when Knox got involved." Clem's face lights up talking about him.

"He has Boone's eyes, but I see you in him. He loves and adores each and every one of you." I can feel the love flowing from this family. It makes me feel warmth like I've never felt.

Nita brings my food to the table. I feel awkward because everyone else's plates are empty. "Could I just get a box to go?" Nita smiles and takes it back to the kitchen.

"Where are you staying?" Molly asks.

"I saw a lodge at the edge of town."

"Don't be silly. You'll stay with us," Clem says.

"How long are you in town for?" Margret places her hand over mine.

"Oh, I'm... I haven't decided," I finally say.

"You can come camping with me and Grandpa." Granger bounces in his seat.

"I'll be fine at the lodge. I don't want to impose on anyone."

"It's not an imposition. We have plenty of room, and we'd love to get to know you." Clem stands, and so does everyone else. "I'll make dinner for everyone tomorrow night. You can meet the entire Calhoun clan."

We walk outside the cafe. "Where are you parked?" Boone asks.

I point to the rental car.

"Nice, but not the greatest car for the ranch. Give me the keys, and I'll have one of our men return it. You won't need wheels." He takes me by the elbow, leads me to a truck, and opens the door. Granger goes to hop in the back, but Boone stops him. "You ride with Grandma. I'd like to spend a little time with our guest."

He stomps off as if he ain't happy about it at all.

Boone marches across the street, grabbing my bags out of the car. I climb in, and he runs to the passenger side, tossing my items in the cab. He settles behind the wheel but doesn't start it. "Does River know you're here?" he asks.

I hang my head and clasp my hands in my lap. "No." I breathe out.

"Getting in the middle of things ain't my thing, but you're fixing to be swarmed by a million questions. I suggest sooner rather than later, you give him a call before someone else does." He starts the diesel engine.

As he drives, I notice how clean his truck is for a rancher. His tidy skills didn't rub off on his son. There's no dust on the dash and not one scrap of trash on the floor. Not even empty water bottles that River seems to collect. And thank goodness his air conditioner works in this heat. His running boards were even shiny when I climbed inside. It doesn't have the stench of exhaust and old food.

I enjoy the drive through the small town. Pedestrians stroll along, saying hello to one another. The businesses are well-tended, with striped awnings shading the storefronts. Light posts with hooks hold colorful flower baskets. Sapling trees are spaced out along sidewalks. There are even water bowls for thirsty dogs placed by business entryways. The entire town feels welcoming, kinda like Missoula used to feel before my father got his claws into it.

"I see why River had a hard time leaving this

place," I say, peering out the window. "It's beautiful, and he has such an amazing family."

"He does, but life wasn't too kind to him here. As much as his mother and I hated to see him leave, it was for the best. I'm so proud of him for building his own life with his son."

"You've raised a good man."

"We all had a hand in raising him," he says, turning out of town, headed for Whiskey River Road.

"You don't take enough credit. Why is that? River is the same way when it comes to Granger." I shift to face him.

"I believe it takes a family to raise someone, not just one or two people. Every one of the Calhouns has impacted his life. His momma and I were there to help him along his way."

He turns onto the dirt road, and the truck bounces, hitting a rut before he drives under the ranch sign. He drives past the main house I saw from the road to the back of the property, where there is a beautiful river flowing through the hills. "This is our house, where River grew up," he says, parking the truck.

Opening the heavy door, I get out, smelling the clean, fresh air like that of Montana. "This place is stunning."

"It's home," he says in his deep voice.

"River was talking about Knox building houses on the property like this. I think it's a great idea for each of them to have their own place."

He opens the door to the rustic-style home that's decorated in farm-style decor. Simple, yet elegant. It suits him.

"Come on in and make yourself at home," Clem says when she sees me.

"Where's Granger?" I ask, thinking he'd be at my feet.

"Deacon, Ellie's son, was headed out on a horse. I sent Granger with him so we could have some girl time."

I don't share with her I met Deacon earlier today when I was stalking this place.

"That's my cue to leave, being I ain't got girl parts." Boone laughs, kissing her on the cheek. "I'm going to check on the cattle. I'll be back in time to snuggle with you." He smiles, using a gravelly voice.

"Behave," she says, grinning.

"Love you," he says, patting her on the ass before he leaves.

"How long have you two been married?" I don't

recall a time when my parents were ever affectionate with one another.

"A very long time." She holds her hand out for me to take a seat on the cushy leather couch. "Did River ever tell you I left Boone at the altar?"

"What? No way!" I howl.

"We almost didn't happen." She sits in a plaid chair. "I was young and wanted to experience life. This place was all I'd ever known. Turns out, it was all I ever needed. I'm grateful every day of my life that Boone gave me a second chance. There's no one else I'd choose to share this life with over him."

I find my eyes watering. "That's an amazing love story. River is so lucky to have parents like you."

She leans her elbows on her knees. "When my husband asked you what you were doing here, you didn't answer. I can assume you weren't just passing through Kentucky."

My lip quivers. "I needed to get away. I'm not exactly sure why I'm here, but I needed to meet a family like yours."

"Does River know you're here?"

I shake my head and wipe my tears. "I don't think he wanted me around. My family has done nothing but cause him trouble."

She scoots off the chair and wedges beside me,

wrapping her arm around my shoulder. "River has never been one to shy away from trouble. When it comes to love, he loves with his whole heart if you're lucky enough for him to let you in. He's guarded it for so long that I can promise you if he cares about you, he's not going to let that go."

"But he didn't try to stop me from leaving," I sniff.

"Sometimes, men can be a little hard-headed. Perhaps he just needed time to put the pieces together."

"I'm not good for him," I cry.

"Why would you say such a thing?"

"My family isn't like yours. They are hurtful people and are only out for themselves."

"Oh, sweetie, I'm so sorry. No wonder you ended up in Salt Lick."

"You don't even know me, but you've made me feel so welcomed and loved. I don't have that with my family."

She grasps both sides of my face. "You look at me. You are a beautiful woman, and I don't have to have known you very long to see your soul is equally as adoring. If my son loves you, I have no doubt you're deserving of it. He learned a hard lesson years ago when it comes to giving your heart to the wrong person. It took him years and a lot of heartache to work his way through it. I'd say if he found you, he's finally healed. And for that, I'm eternally grateful."

I cry on her shoulder.

"I'm going to step out and check on my grandson. It will give you a chance to call River." She kisses my cheek and pushes off the couch.

"Clem," I say before she opens the door.

She turns to face me.

"Thank you for being such a kind woman. I'm glad Boone gave you another chance too."

"Boone put your bags in that room." She points. "Make yourself at home."

CHAPTER FIVE
RIVER

"The last time I went to a bar, you had to haul my ass out." Chase looks solemn as we meander through the swinging doors of the brewery.

We settle on two stools in the middle so that we can see everyone coming and going and we can be heard.

"What can I get you, gentleman?" the bartender asks, laying tan napkins with the brewery's logo on them on the counter.

"I'll take whatever is on draft and isn't hoppy," I say.

"Seltzer water and a lime," Chase orders.

Blaise ambles in, and three women sharing a table all sweep their heads in his direction, drooling.

He smiles and pulls out a chair in between them. Scanning the bar, he gives a slight nod in my direction, then carries on with the women.

"He's such a horn dog," Chase grumbles

"The ladies love him."

He leans on the bar, hanging his head.

"If this is too much for you, we can leave," I say, seeing he's struggling.

He raises his head, and his jaw visibly flexes. "No, I'm good. We need to get this handled tonight."

"I'm always here for you if you need to talk. I know you hold things in, but if you'd like to get things off your chest, you know I'll listen without judgment, just as you've done for me."

"I appreciate it, man." He claps his hand on my back. "I'm good. Let's get this done so you can work on finding Greer."

Country music plays over the speaker, and more patrons arrive as the night goes on. Lance sashays in as if he owns the place with a woman on each arm. The smug look on his face says he's ready for a cockfight.

"It's showtime," I tell Chase, taking one last swig of my beer.

"Looks like the people of this town have voted to oust Sheriff Grady," he says ear-splittingly loud.

"Old man Alden is next. We'll clean up this town and run off him and his sons." I angle, so Lance will be sure to hear me.

He brushes the woman off his arm and storms toward me, knocking over an empty chair. "What is it you're mouthing off about, Methany!" He spits my name from his mouth, with his nostrils flaring, holding his elbows out wide and thrusting out his chest.

"I filed the petition with the courthouse today to have Grady removed from office." Chase stands nose to nose with him.

Lance snorts. "My father will never allow that to happen. Keep running your mouth, and you're likely to find yourself in more trouble than you bargained for." He bumps his chest into Chase like a rooster, showing its tail feathers.

"You need to back the hell off!" I shove him.

He catches himself on the bar. Standing, straightening his spine, he cracks his neck from side to side. "You don't know who you've done pissed off." He spits on the wooden floor. "I don't know what my sister sees in you other than your pretty boy looks. You're a loser who killed a woman!" He says the last part vehemently, and ladies in close proximity gasp.

Chase moves to topple Lance, and I step in front

of him, holding him back. "He spews lies, nothing more. This coming from a bully, owned and controlled by his father."

"No one owns me!" he spats with a snarl. "You can either stay in here and get your ass whooped, or we can take it outside." He's in my face with his lips twitching.

"It takes a big man to fight when he can't choose his words," I scoff, egging him on.

"Are you calling me stupid?" he rages.

"If the cowboy boots fit." I shrug nonchalantly.

He spins around, purposely throwing a stool to the ground and pushing people in his way to get outside.

"Are you ready?" I mouth to Blaise.

He stands, tips his hat to the ladies who are batting their lashes at him, and exits through the back door.

I pay the bar tab and follow Chase outside, moseying to his truck. He unlocks the door and casually reaches inside, taking out two cigars and handing me one.

"The last time I smoked one of these, I puked." I chuckle as he lights it.

"You had a bad one. These are good," he says,

sucking on the end of it, then blowing out a ring of smoke.

Letting down the tailgate, I sit, and Chase leans against it with his feet crossed at the ankles as if he ain't got a care in the world. "How long do you think before he shows up?" I puff on the cigar, enjoying the sweet taste.

"I'd say right about... now." He cuts his gaze to the side where Lance has something grasped in his right hand behind his back, stomping toward us with steam coming out of his ears and baring his teeth.

"You're lucky I couldn't locate your son, or I'd have killed him first and made you watch." His eyes are tight and cold, and his body is tense, with a vein pulsating on the side of his neck.

He gets within steps of me and strikes out with a six-inch shiny knife. Chase leans to the side, raises his leg in the air, and kicks it out of his hand, with his boot laying a powerful kick, snapping Lance's wrist.

He cries out in pain. "I'm going to kill both of you!" he wails.

"Did you get it on video?" I ask as Blaise approaches, and Chase calls the police.

"I did." He shows me and turns up the volume.

Lance tries to run, but I tackle him to the ground, pinning his uninjured arm behind him, nailing my knee to the center of his back. "Your days of running buckshot over this town are done."

"Get the hell off of me!" he squawks.

"You're not going anywhere but to jail."

"My father will have me out with one phone call, and I'm going to finish what I started. You won't see another day!"

Chase bends down, grabbing him by the hair, and twisting his head so Lance can look in his face. "I'm betting your father is going to let your sorry, miserable ass rot in jail this time. He'll see this video and won't want to be connected to you. Proof is a powerful tool."

"You're wrong! He'll bail me out!" His face is red as he yells.

I keep him pinned until blue lights park beside us. A Missoula police officer steps out and then halts when Sheriff Grady skids to a stop next to him. "I'll handle this," he growls, flinging his door open.

"You might want to wait a minute," Chase tells the cop.

"How come you're manhandling Alden's son, boy?" Grady spats in my face, tucking his thumbs in his belt.

"Show him the video of Lance trying to kill me." I motion to Blaise.

He hits play and puts it on full volume so the police officer can hear it too.

He steps up next to Grady, who's gnawing on the inside of his cheek. "Seems like you've left me no choice," he says, getting Lance to his feet. "You're under arrest."

"He broke my wrist!" Lance shouts. "He attacked me first. The big guy is the one that needs to be arrested."

Grady lets go of Lance and moves toward Chase, who stands tall with his feet wide apart and his arms crossed over his chest. The cop intervenes with a hand on Grady's shoulder. "That's not going to happen. It was clear on the video it was a self-defense move. You'd be wise to do the right thing in this situation." His voice is deep and commanding.

Grady backs down, returning to Lance, shoving him toward his cruiser. "This one is out of my hands, son."

"Get my father on the phone!" Lance shrieks, his eyes bulging.

"Thanks for your help, Officer." Chase shakes his hand.

"Knowing Grady, he'll find a way to get Lance out

of this mess. He's as dirty as they come. I can only hope the petition that was going around gets him kicked out."

"You signed it?" I ask quizzically.

"I'd love nothing more than to have Alden run out of town." He shakes Chase's hand and returns to his police car.

"That was too easy," I say, picking up the cigar I laid on the tailgate.

"The fight has just begun. Just because we subdued Lance, for now, doesn't mean there's not more raining down on us." He shuts the tailgate.

"Great job." I slap Blaise on the back. "Did you get the part where he threatened Granger?"

"I sure did. I saved that sweet bit of info in case we need more ammo against him."

"We're going to head to the sheriff's office to make sure he keeps Lance where he belongs. Do you want to join us?"

He hits send on his phone, giving me the video. "Nah. There are three pretty ladies inside I'd like to get to know a little better, if you know what I mean." He winks.

"Go have fun, and stay out of trouble." I chuckle.

"And for land's sake, don't be silly, wrap your willy," Chase hollers, and I roar out laughing.

"You've been hanging around Knox way too much," I say, planting my boot on his muddy running board.

We roll down the windows, letting the cigar smoke float into the darkness of the night as we drive the short distance to Grady's office. Lance is in the holding cell, swearing like a sailor.

"You let me talk to him! I ain't spending the night in this place!" He sticks his chin in the air, then cracks his knuckles.

"I'm sorry, boy, but I just hung up with him. He said he ain't dealing with this crap until morning."

"I'll have formal charges filed by then," I say, walking over to the cell.

"Make this go away!" Lance snarls, looking over my shoulder with his fingers turning white from gripping the bars.

Chase storms in front of Grady's desk. "The petition signed by almost the entire town to have you removed from office was presented to the authorities today. I'd say you have about ten days before you lose that shiny silver badge of yours." He taps the center of the badge with his index finger.

"Are you threatening me, son?" he snaps.

"Simply stating the facts." Chase turns toward

me. "I'll look mighty damn good sitting behind that desk."

"Nah, that desk ain't good enough for you. You need something bigger and sturdier." I pound my fist on it.

"Get out!" Grady yells and points to the door.

"You have yourself a good night." I tip my hat and smirk.

He flexes his jaw and balls his hands into fists. "You have any idea where Alden's daughter is?"

I whip my head in his direction and stiffen. "What does she have to do with any of this?"

"She's always been the pawn between me and Alden. If I lose my job, his daughter will go missing."

I fly over the desk, wrapping my hands around his throat, wanting nothing more than to squeeze the life out of him for his threats to Greer.

Chase grabs me by the ankles, prying me off of him. "He ain't worth killing," he growls. I get to my feet, and Chase's body blocks mine. "He ain't gonna lay one hand on Greer if he values his life and badge at all. I might not let my cousin end your life, but I got no problem doing it myself and making it look like an accident." Chase's tone is even menacing to me.

Grady swallows hard. "Get out of my office."

Chase grips my shoulder hard, dragging me out of the building. "Don't let him get to you. He's not going to touch Greer."

"How do you know that for sure?" I jerk free of his hold.

"Because by the time we find her, he'll be long gone. He knows too many of Alden's secrets for him to let him hang around."

"Do you think Alden will have Grady killed?"

"That would be my bet because if Grady is a vengeful man, he'll be out to destroy the Alden family. I'm sure he knows all of their skeletons and will be more than happy to use it against him."

"I guess that's where the phrase 'keep your enemies closer' comes into play. If we're lucky, they'll take each other down. The issue will be how to keep Greer from going down with them."

CHAPTER SIX

GREER

When Clem shuts the door, I snatch my phone from my purse and walk into the spare bedroom where Boone set my bags next to the vintage maple dresser. Sitting on the edge of the bed, I tap a loose fist to my lips, searching for the last call I received. It's from Mercy, not River. I debate with myself which one to call. Perhaps something happened to River. My heart races, and I slow it down, taking a deep breath, then slowly blowing it out. I decide to call Mercy. It rings twice when she picks up.

"Where are you?" she asks.

"I'm... is River alright?" My nails clang on my teeth, drumming them.

"He's beside himself with worry."

"He hasn't called me."

"He used my phone. He had some mishap with his, and it got crushed."

"He didn't leave me a voicemail."

"More than likely, he didn't know what to say." She sighs. "Are you okay?"

"I wasn't, but I'm better now."

"River tried to go after you. Knox found him broken down on the side of the road in a tizzy, trying to get to you."

"Really?" I ask, surprised.

"Yes, really. Wherever you are, would you please come home? We're all worried about you."

"I'm not ready yet. I need a little more time."

"Then at least call him. He's with Chase. I'll text you his number. Better yet, he just walked in the door. I'll give him my phone."

I can hear her whispering to him.

"Greer," his voice sounds raspy. "Where are you? I'm so sorry for not answering you right. I'm an idiot. Please forgive me."

"There's nothing to forgive. I should've given you time to respond."

"My dang truck wouldn't start. Knox showed up, and we went to your aunt's house. Your mother told me you went to the airport, so I did too. I saw you and yelled your name right before you made it to your gate."

"You did?" He did come after me.

"Yes. You were listening to music or something and didn't hear me. They wouldn't let me past security to come get you."

I'm quiet, taking in what he's saying.

"I love you, Greer. That should've been the only thing out of my mouth, and I'm sorry that it wasn't."

I gulp, and tears flood my eyes. "Thank you for telling me. I know how hard it is for you to use those words."

"I'll tell you every single day if you'll come home."

I bite my lip. "I'm in Salt Lick."

"What?"

"It wasn't my plan, but it hit me on the plane. I wanted to meet your family. Well, not actually meet them, but see who they were. Turns out, Salt Lick is one of those small towns where everyone knows everyone. I ended up at your aunt's cafe. All the women in your family were there. I was enjoying listening to their conversation without them knowing who I was until your dad and Granger showed up. Your family's a hoot, by the way. I see where Knox gets her dirty mind," I add, giggling.

"I can't believe you're in my hometown." I can hear him scratching his chin.

"At this very moment, I'm in the house you grew up in."

"Which bedroom?" His voice grows husky.

"It has navy and white walls with two windows."

"That's my old room," he says.

"Ah, that's why your father brought my suitcases in here." I lie back on the bed. "Are you angry I'm here?"

"Not if it's made you feel better."

"Just for one moment of my life, I wanted to know how it felt to be loved like you by your family."

"And?"

"It's a wonderful feeling. From the moment I met them, I could feel it."

"Good. Stay a couple of days, then bring my son home with you."

"Does that mean the danger is over?" I sit tall.

His deep inhale is loud. "Lance is behind bars. He tried to kill me tonight and threatened my son."

I gasp, covering my mouth with my hand. "Are you alright? Did he hurt you?"

"He never laid a hand on me. Chase stopped him and broke his wrist. Blaise videoed the encounter, so there's no disputing what happened.

Your father won't be able to get him out of this one."

"You set him up, didn't you?"

"I won't lie to you. Yes, I did. Are you mad?"

"Not at all. It's about time someone put him in his place. Maybe once he sees he won't get away with it, he'll change his ways."

"I wish you were here so I could hold you in my arms."

"You'll have to settle for knowing I'm in your bed in the house you grew up in." I lie back down, running my hand over the covers.

"No woman has ever been in that bed with me, much less that room."

"Seriously? You never snuck some girl through the windows," I snicker.

"Not one. My daddy would have shot me. Besides, I respected my parents too much to do such a thing. But that leaves me suspicious of you when you were a teenager." He laughs.

"We won't go there," I snort.

"The petition you started was overflowing with signatures. Chase filed the paperwork today to get the ball rolling on removing Grady."

"My father is going to be ticked off. You need to watch your back more than ever."

"I've got that part handled, but there's more."

"I'm afraid to ask."

"Grady said you were the pawn between him and your father all these years."

My mind reels with what he said.

"You working for him has kept Grady away from you. It was your father's security net. He controlled both the people who knew his secrets. I'm afraid you're more in danger than ever before. When you come back with Granger, I want you under my roof where I can protect you."

"If your only reason for me to live there is to protect me, then no thanks," I snap.

"Gah, that's not what I meant. That's only part of the reason."

"Then say what you mean."

"I didn't want to fall in love with you, but at some point, you blew me away, and I had no choice. I want late-night dinners with you underneath the stars. To cuddle with you in my arms. To hear your laughter at two in the morning and to be your pillow when you sleep. You are the moon and stars for me." His voice is low and sexy.

My body heat rises. "For a man of few words, I'd say each and every one of them was perfect." I lay my hand over my heart, feeling it pound.

"Then you'll come home to me?" he asks with hope mingled in his voice.

"Yes," I rasp. "When I'm ready, I'll come home to you."

"Give my little man a hug for me. It's been a really long day, and now that I know where you are, I can finally sleep," he says with a yawn.

"Good night. I love you," I say softly, wanting to hear him tell me one more time.

"I love you with all my heart. Come home soon." He hangs up.

I fall fast asleep to his words.

ONE EYE CRACKS OPEN, squinting at my surroundings, forgetting for a moment where I am. I'm lying cross-wise on the bed, still dressed in my clothes from yesterday. Grabbing one pillow, I cuddle it to my chest, knowing River once slept on it. A smile covers my face with a feeling of happiness. My phone pings next to me with a text message.

GOOD MORNING, *beautiful. I wanted you to start your day knowing that I love you.*

. . .

I TOSS the pillow over my smile and laugh hard. "He loves me!" I yell into it, feeling like a girl swooning over a boy. Rolling to my side, I respond to his text.

GOOD MORNING, cowboy. Thank you for your sweet message. I love you, too.

A KNOCK on the door has me sitting tall.

"Breakfast is ready if you'd like to join us," Clem says without opening it.

I jump to my feet and unzip my suitcase to find a fresh set of clothes. Quickly dressing, I run a brush through my knotted hair and braid it to the side. Patting a dab of lip gloss on my finger, I apply it to my dry lips, then slip on my boots, bolting out of the room.

Boone is sitting at the head of the table, sipping on coffee, and Granger is shoveling pancakes into his mouth while talking. "Can you take me horse-back riding today?"

"You smell like a horse," Clem says, setting a plate of food on the table.

"When's the last time you bathed?" Boone runs his fingers through Granger's hair.

"Cowboys don't bathe," he says, sniffing his pits.

"On this ranch, they do." Clem laughs.

"Girls don't like smelly cowboys," I say, sitting next to him.

"Did you and Daddy make up, or are we a thing again?" He bats his eyes.

"Are you sure you're only eight years old?" I snort.

"Eight going on sixteen." Clem giggles, settling next to her husband.

"After you're cleaned up, we can go on a ride," Boone tells him.

"I'll just get stinky again." He rolls his eyes, and Boone cocks a disapproving brow at him. "Alright. I'll get a bath," he concedes.

"Would you mind if I tagged along?" I ask, wanting to see the land up close and personal.

"That would be awesome," Granger shouts. "Please, Grandpa, can she come with us?"

"Sure she can. You do know how to ride a horse?" He tilts his head toward me.

"I've been riding since I was about Granger's age."

"Good because I'm too old to be teaching people how to ride."

"Too cranky too." Clem squeezes his hand and winks at him.

"River told me over dinner one night that the two of you were trainers, and you've had several horses and riders in the derbies." I pick up the platter of homemade biscuits, and set one on my plate, then butter it.

"Boone still dabbles in it. I gave it up when River hit his teenage years. He had too much going on for me to focus on anything else."

"What was he like as a kid?" I say, slathering honey on my biscuit.

Clem points to Boone. "Just like him. A pain in my arse." She speaks out of the side of her mouth.

"He was hard-headed like his momma but a good kid." Boone takes a bite of his crispy bacon.

"I bet he was adorable," I snort.

"Like me," Granger says, grinning.

"Just like you." Clem laughs.

Granger snaps out of his chair and rinses off his plate before he places it in the dishwasher. He runs toward his bedroom.

"Make sure you use soap," Clem hollers.

"He's such a sweet kid. River has done a good job

with him." I bite my biscuit. "Oh my, gosh. This is so good. You'll have to give me your recipe." I wipe the drip of honey from my chin with the back of my hand.

"These are River's favorite. I'll be happy to share it with you." Clem hands me a napkin. "Do you need anything from town? I've got to run a few errands."

"I'm good, thanks."

"Did you let River know you're here?" Boone glances at me.

"Yes, sir. We're all good."

"I spoke with him this morning," Clem tells him. "He said when Greer is ready to go back, we're to send Granger with her."

"It will save me a trip. Ethan and I are scheduled to take the cattle to auction."

"You should come for a visit," I tell Clem.

"Cattle selling time is busy for all of us. River will be doing the same thing. Once the season is over, I'll come, don't you worry. I miss my boy."

"I'm sure you do, but I promise I'll take good care of both of them for you."

CHAPTER SEVEN
RIVER

*G*ood morning, cowboy. Thank you for your sweet message. I love you, too.

GREER'S TEXT makes me smile.

"Why are you grinning like a possum?" Mercy asks, walking past me.

"Do possum's grin?" I chuckle.

She slaps her hand on her hip. "I have no earthly idea. It's something Aunt Ellie used to say."

The radio on the counter cracks with Walker's voice. "Alden is parked out at the entrance of the ranch with a few men."

Hustling to my rifle, I fist it in my hand. "Stay

inside the house," I grumble at Mercy. Copper comes flying down the stairs, barking with his hair standing on end.

"Sit," I command. "Stay." I make eye contact with him so he knows I mean business. "Don't let him out. Alden's likely to shoot him if he feels threatened," I tell Mercy before opening the door.

Chase meets me out front, and we hop on the four-wheelers, riding them to the entrance. Alden is in his usually stuffy suit, with a man on either side of him, bracing guns, and two more men near his car carrying clipboards.

"Get off my property," I bellow, stomping over to him with Chase glaring over my shoulder.

"Your property line doesn't reach this part of the dirt," he scoffs.

"What do you want?" Walker scoots in front of me.

"What do I want?" He anchors an elbow on his gut and taps a finger to his lips. "For starters, you erase the video of my son that makes it appear he was doing some injustice."

"Not going to happen," Chase chimes in.

"No matter." He waves dismissively. "My attorney will prove it was nothing more than a setup." He takes a step closer to me. "If you have Grady removed from office, you're putting my precious daughter's life in danger. I don't think you want another woman's death linked to you, do you now, boy?"

I hand Chase my rifle, sticking my hands deep inside my jean pockets so as not to strangle him again. "No harm will come to Greer," I say with confidence. "As far as your insinuation, nobody will ever believe I'd hurt her. I'd never lay a hand on a woman, regardless of the rumors you've spread." I moved away from home because of what people thought of me. I won't be run off again.

He turns, facing the two men that are standing next to him. "This will be my property soon. It's your job to get this land surveyed. I have already proven it encroaches mine. I want every inch that belongs to me on record." He spins around. "I'll pay you ten million for this land. It's more than it's worth, and I'm only offering it one time." He holds up a single digit in my face.

"You can stick your offer where the sun don't shine," Walker growls.

"I wasn't speaking to you, boy," Alden snarls

I bare my teeth. "Your biscuit ain't done in the middle, and I'm having a hard time overlooking it. These are my stompin' grounds, and they ain't for sale for any amount of money." I go nose to nose with him, leaving my hands in my pockets. "Do I make myself clear?" Spittle flies in his face.

"You've made a huge mistake, boy." He wipes his face on his sleeve, taking a step back. "If any post is a smidgen on my property, I want it torn down. If a cow has its head hanging on my side or its tail swishes over the barbed wire, I want it shot and taken to the butcher to be put in my freezer. I'm done playing nice with you, Methany." He turns around and gets in his car. The men holding clipboards take out their gear.

"If he's been nice, I'd sure hate to see his sweet side," Walker mutters.

Chase storms over to the surveyors. "You can follow him down the dirt road. You ain't coming on this land, and if I catch you on it, trespassers will be shot just like the posted signs say."

They mumble among themselves, then throw their gear back in the trunk and drive off, leaving dust flying in the air.

"I'll make some calls to see that Lance is still in a cell." Chase marches off.

"What do you need from me?" Walker asks.

"Keep protecting the house. I doubt he'll make another move today. Put men on every corner of the property, and bring the cattle into the inner pastures for grazing. They go to auction tomorrow, and I don't want to risk Alden going through with his threat and losing one of them." It took every ounce of my energy not to lose my temper with him. I want to think he's all talk and just baiting me, but I can't take the chance on it.

Mercy is on the porch with a leash on Copper when I return to the house. "Why are you out here instead of inside?"

"Copper was going to eat through the door, so instead of letting him, I chose to leash him. He calmed down when he could see you."

I squat. "Sorry, boy. It was for your own good."

Chase bounds out of the house. "Lance is still in custody. A judge who apparently got wind of the petition against Grady decided on no bail for his son. He said it was about time the man was held accountable for his crimes."

"Oh, how the tides are changing," I say, grinning.

"Yeah, well, the more we piss off Alden, trouble is going to continue to show up on our doorstep."

"Apparently, you were right. Alden told the judge he didn't order Lance to go after you and that he's ashamed of his boy for doing so."

"He's all bluster then, saying he'd have his attorney change the narrative of the video." I stand.

"What do you think his next move will be?"

"I'm sure he'll try to bribe someone," Mercy snorts.

"He'll come after Greer once he finds out she'll be living here with me."

"I'm so proud of you." Mercy high-fives me. "You actually took my advice. Wait." She frowns. "She did say yes, right?"

"I laid the charm on just like you told me, and she ate it up. Thanks for the advice."

"Did you find out where she ran off to?"

"She's with my mom and dad."

"How the heck did that happen?" She laughs.

"Long story, but I'm glad she's there. They all made her feel welcomed, and that's something she needed."

"When's she coming home?"

"She wanted a little more time. When she does come back, she'll bring Granger with her."

We all keep our radios attached to our hips throughout the evening, staying on high alert. I check in with Granger and spend an hour on the phone with Greer. She had a great time riding horses with my dad and son.

I go to bed and wake up early, loading the cattle for auction. Chase goes to climb into the truck, but I stop him. "You may not like it, but I need you to stay here and guard the house. Walker and I can handle it from here."

"You're right. I don't like it, but I get it," he grumbles.

"Uncle Ethan will be on the phone with me. He's already done the research on cattle sales in this area. He'll walk me through any questions I might have, and he'll help me get the best price per head. Have Blaise get a head count on our younger cattle that remain. We'll need to purchase a few more bulls."

"I've got a line on the bulls, and I'll make sure the head count is done by the end of the day. There are a few more calfs that need branding with the Methany M. Knox is in charge of it."

"Sounds like everything is falling into place. With the sale of the cattle, Knox can turn in the blueprints we had made and start building houses."

"Not that I'm unappreciative, but it will be nice to have my own space."

"I agree." I chuckle. "It's hard living with two women you ain't married to, but I'm grateful."

THE AUCTION IS BUSY. Every rancher in town is here seeking the highest bid. I stop and register my name and cattle on the list at the table.

"Methany Ranch," the man holding my paperwork reads. "I heard your cattle weren't fit for market. Word is they've been ill."

"Let me guess. Alden's been spreading rumors." I show him the cattle's medical records, clearing them of all diseases.

"This looks official to me," he says, stamping my registration.

"Bastard," Walker growls. "He'll do anything to see to it you fail."

"Failure is not an option." We move into the stadium, where the cattle have already been offloaded and are in a holding pen outside, ready to be brought in once the auction gets underway.

Alden struts in as if he owns the place, with his goons by his side. He sits three rows down from us. He glares at me, snarling before he takes his seat.

The announcer comes on, and I dial up Uncle Ethan. "It's started," I tell him.

"I've contacted an old friend. He's registered as a buyer under the name Texas Beef. They've already researched your cattle, and he'll give you the highest bid."

"Alden spread rumors that my cattle had been sick and weren't fit for consumption."

"Let him. It won't hinder the sale," he says. "Let me know if there are any issues. I'll keep my phone handy."

"Thanks for your help." I hang up.

The buyers start their bidding as the cattle are paraded through. One company raises their bid card to bid on my cattle, and Alden motions for one of his men to go over to him. He whispers something to the guy, and he shakes his head, withdrawing the bid.

Alden spins his head around and plasters on an ugly fake smile. Walker shuffles his feet to stand, and I grab his arm. "Don't. He's not going to win."

Texas Beef holds up his card along with a number that's a substantial bid higher than what I was expecting and more than others have been on other ranches.

Alden's face turns red, and he sends two men over to where Texas Beef is sitting. The owner shakes them off, telling them to move out of his view. They stand side by side with their arms crossed, directly in front of him, not budging.

The owner simply waves for security to remove them. Alden stomps his feet like a two-year-old child not getting his way. "You're going to regret buying his cattle!" he seethes, yelling at him.

Walker and I rest back in our stadium seats with smug looks. We could leave, but I want to stick around and see the price Alden gets for his herd.

The bidding continues, and buyers are staying clear of the Alden name. I can see him getting angrier and angrier by the minute. His eyes protrude, and his lips flatten as he rolls up his sleeves. He snaps at one of his men, shaking his fist.

A buyer holds up his card with a lowball bid, and Alden flips a gasket, yelling across the stadium. "That's a pathetic bid! I won't give away my cattle!"

"I think it's time for us to get out of here." I stand, leading the way.

"Boy howdy is he pissed" Walker laughs.

"His reputation is finally catching up with him. It's his own fault for the way he's treated everyone, including his family."

"You did good, cousin. You made a lot more than you thought you would."

"Thanks to Uncle Ethan. Let's get on the road before Alden comes looking for us."

CHAPTER EIGHT
GREER

"We sure are going to miss the two of you." Clem hugs my neck.

"I can't thank you enough for your hospitality and for not throwing me out when I showed up in town."

"You're welcome here anytime you need," she says.

"Your family as far as we're concerned," Boone adds, picking up Granger to give him one more hug before he gets on the plane.

"Give my boy a kiss for me." Clem gets teary-eyed.

"I will. I promise." Extending the handle on my suitcase, I position it to roll. Boone puts Granger on his feet, and he grabs my hand and adjusts his backpack.

"I miss you already," he says in his sweet little voice, making Clem swipe away tears.

"We love you, little man. We'll come out to see you soon." Boone kisses the top of his head.

He gives us a final wave as we go through security to our gate. Boone upgraded our tickets to first class, so we're sitting in the very first row. Granger makes himself comfortable with his new handheld gaming console his grandpa bought him for the flight. I take out my phone to turn it on airplane mode and see I have several text messages from my father, demanding I come home. He's ranting about the family being in trouble financially, and it's all my fault. I delete every single one of them without another thought, knowing he's being overly dramatic and trying to control me.

"I know you're going to miss your grandma and grandpa, but are you excited about going home?" I make sure his seat belt is snug.

"Yes," he says, nodding, not taking his eyes off his game.

I guess it will be a quiet flight. Who can blame him at his age? Before I put my phone away, I text River one last time.

. . .

WE'RE ON BOARD. Only a few short hours now until I can hold you in my arms. As much as I've enjoyed getting to know your family, I've missed you. See you soon.

WE'VE SPENT a lot of time the past few days texting one another and sharing midnight calls. I've told him all about my days on the ranch and getting to know each of his family members. The dinner we had all together was the best. None of them hold anything back, and they are so real and hilarious. I love the fact that even at their ages, the women have dirty minds, and the men eat it up. I even learned a few naughty terms for body parts I'd never heard. They were all so loving and supportive of each other, and I fell in love with each of them. River and I have a lot of things to work out. I only pray that we turn out like his family.

River would listen to me for hours on the phone and tell me the simple things that went on during his days, but he never mentioned a word about my father or my brother, and I'm thankful. The break has done me good, and the bond we've built between us has strengthened me. There are no more doubts about whether or not he loves me. Especially when he told me I was his moon and stars. I know what that tattoo means to him. He's kept his promise and told me every day how much he loves and wants me. Me... Greer. Not Alden's daughter. Not for what my name will do for someone. Just me. A woman who finally has a chance at having a simple, meaningful life.

It's funny to think I left a week ago, desperate to run away from my life, and now, I'm running toward it with open arms, thanks to feeling loved by strangers who I long to call family.

Granger is in heaven the entire flight and whines when we land, not wanting to tuck away his game. "Can't I play one more time?"

"Put it in your bag. We're getting off the plane, and I'll need you to hold my hand walking through the airport, so I don't get lost." He loves feeling useful.

"Okay," he says, stuffing the game in one of the side pockets.

He smiles the entire time he holds my hand in his. "Daddy's going to be so jealous when he sees us together," he says, beaming up at me.

"Yes, he is." I giggle.

As soon as we walk out of the airport doors,

Granger sees River sitting on the tailgate of a shiny new, navy-colored Dodge truck. "Is this yours?" he squeals, jumping into his father's arms.

"It sure is," he roars.

"You finally did it," I say, kissing him.

"I don't ever want to not be able to chase you down again." He laughs, grabbing my suitcase. He puts it in the back, sets Granger down, and shuts the tailgate.

"Are you happy to see me, even though I came back with my girlfriend?" Granger is wearing a cheesy grin.

"About that." River squats. "I know how much you care about her, but I'm in love with her, and she is more my age than yours. So, what would you say to giving her up for me?"

He props his hand on his hip. "Do I still get to spend time with her?"

"Absolutely. I've asked her to move into the house with us."

"In the spare room?" His eyes grow large.

River glances up at me. "Um... I was thinking mine if you'd be okay with that."

He looks at her, then at me. "What if I have a nightmare? Who's going to help me?"

"We both will," I assure him, placing my hand on his head.

"Then I guess it's alright." He blinks his eyes several times. "Besides, there's a cute girl in my class I've been keeping my eye on." We both crack up at his facial expression.

River stands. "Now that we have that settled, let's go home." He places his hand on the small of my back, opening the door.

"I like your truck, cowboy." I wink.

Granger jumps in the middle and smiles. "Can I drive, Daddy?"

River runs to the driver's side. The new leather creaks as he settles behind the wheel. "Not until you're older, son."

"Grandpa let me drive the tractor, sitting in his lap. I wasn't tall enough to reach the pedals."

"How about I teach you how to drive the four-wheeler in the pasture first?"

"Yay!" He bounces and claps.

The short drive back to Whiskey River West is filled with nonstop talking by Granger, telling his daddy about all the things he did on the Calhoun Ranch. When we park in the driveway, River runs around and opens my door, sporting a handsome smile. He holds out his hand to help me but doesn't release it when my feet are planted firmly on the ground.

"Welcome home." He kisses the back of my hand.

"I'm kinda liking this sweeter side of you," I tease, batting my lashes.

Granger stomps up the steps to the house, rushing inside as River gets our bags. Once inside, Granger repeats all his stories to Mercy and Knox in one breath.

"Sounds like you had a great time." Knox ruffles his hair.

"It's good to have you home." Mercy hugs me. "I've missed you."

"I've missed all of you, too, but it turned out to be one of the best things that's ever happened to me."

"Besides me, you mean." River wraps his arm low on my waist, drawing me into him.

"Of course, besides you, silly," I snicker.

"I've got lunch made. You must be starving." Mercy takes out plates.

"Are you kidding me? I think I've gained ten pounds since I've been gone. Clem is a fantastic cook." I brace my hand on my stomach.

River runs up the stairs with our belongings and

jogs back down. "If you're not going to eat, I'll take you to your aunt's house to get your things."

"It would be nice if I knew where I'll be sleeping," I say, and Mercy snorts.

He turns a pretty shade of pink. "I'm sorry." He takes my hand, leading me up the stairs. "It's the room at the end of the hallway. It's the master suite, so you don't have to share a bathroom with anyone but me." He taps on the door next to his. "This is Granger's room."

River's bedroom has a rustic king-size bed and a matching dresser. No pictures on the wall or anything on his dresser. "I'm not much of a decorator." He shrugs. "Feel free to add whatever you want. Just please don't make it too girly."

Sitting on the bed, I rub the spot next to me. "I think we should pick some things out together that would suit both our needs."

He reaches behind him, slowly shutting the door and locking it. "I've missed you," he rasps.

My lips part, and I fidget with the charm on my necklace while skimming my gaze down his body. "I've missed you touching me," I whisper, itching to have my hands on him.

He swaggers toward me, kicking off his boots one

at a time. "I can remedy that." His voice is smooth as silk.

I peel out of my top, so there is nothing getting in his way. Sliding my hands behind my back, I unfasten my bra. Before I can move, he pins me with my hands underneath me. "We don't have much time before Granger interrupts us, so I'm sorry if this will be quick, but I'll be sure to take care of you." His breath is warm against my neck, making my body temperature rise quickly. Maneuvering my arms, he traps my wrists together above my head with one hand. "Don't move." His pupils dilate with his command.

I pant, licking my lips as he leisurely rises, unfastening my jeans. I remove my own shoes, toeing them off. "Lift your hips," he moans. He easily draws my jeans down my legs, tossing them to the floor. "Remember what I said, don't move."

His arousal is apparent in his tenting blue jeans. He gets to his knees, dipping his head between my legs and pressing his hands on the inside of my thighs to widen them. I hiss when his tongue delves into my tender flesh.

"Mmmm," he says, making my lady parts vibrate. "You taste like peaches." He licks his mouth, and gazes at me, then dives back inside me, moaning and sucking as he inserts a finger. My back bows off the bed, and I fist the sheets above me, trying to keep my hands in place. "Sit still," he barks, coming up for air.

"I can't," I squeal, rocking my hips to the rhythm of his delicious tongue driving me crazy.

He arches up. "Stop." His tone spikes my desire even more.

I quit moving on his command and bite my bottom lip, waiting and wanting whatever it is he has to give to me.

He drags me to the edge of the bed and lowers his head again. I bear his tongue lashing without a peep, but my belly burns, wanting to scream his name. Scissoring his fingers inside me sends me over the edge, panting with desire and pulsating around him and into his mouth. When my body stops convulsing with pure pleasure, he hovers over me with a smile. I didn't realize he'd even moved. I reach for his zipper, and there's a pounding on the door.

"Daddy. You said you'd teach me how to drive the four-wheeler!" Granger yells insistently.

"Welcome home," River says, resting his damp forehead against mine.

"I'll leave and come back again for this anytime."

I drape my arms around his neck, pulling him in for a hard kiss. "I do taste like peaches," I tease.

"Daddy!" Granger hollers and knocks harder.

"I'll make sure to show my appreciation later." I wipe his lips with my fingertips, and he snags them playfully between his teeth.

"I'll hold you to it. Get dressed," he says, grabbing his boots.

"I like this sweet and bossy side of you," I say, picking up my jeans and disappearing into the bathroom.

I hear him tell Granger when he opens the door, "I didn't mean right this minute."

Rummaging through the cabinets, I find a towel and washcloth. The shower is enclosed by glass with gray tile on the floor and walls. Turning the shower head on, I pick up a bottle of generic shampoo. "This will certainly have to change." I chuckle and feel warmth between my legs. My hair drenches underneath the spray of the water, cascading down my backside. The smile I'm wearing may be a permeant thing with the way things are going. Never in my life have I felt such pure joy and at ease with myself. Nothing else in the world matters to me than being here with this family.

Drying off, I unzip my suitcase and slip on a pair

of tattered blue jean shorts and a T-shirt, pulling on my boots. I run downstairs to find River.

"Granger conned him into riding the four-wheeler." Mercy laughs, tugging back the sheers on the living room window to peer out.

Swinging open the front door, I march down the steps and plant myself on the top rung of the fence and watch Granger driving with River on the seat behind him.

"Granger's loving it," Mercy says, joining me. "I'm happy the two of you worked things out. River was a mess, not knowing where you were. You look good on him." She smiles.

"I'm so in love with both of them," I respond. "I never thought I'd honestly fall for a man, much less his son. Right now, there is no place I'd rather be than with these two men." I lay my head on her shoulder.

CHAPTER NINE
RIVER

"It's been five days since our run-in with Alden at the auction. I'm surprised he hasn't made some type of play against us yet." I wipe the sweat from my forehead with the back of my hand. I've peeled out of my shirt because it's hotter than blazes on the roof of the barn.

Chase hammers a nail into a sheet of plywood, covering the area the barn leaked from the storm last night. "He's more than likely thinking we'll get comfortable and let our guard down. That's when he'll attack us."

"As long as everything is up in the air, I'm not letting up on anything we have in place. Have you heard on the petition yet on Grady?"

"I know it's been approved and will be going

through in the next couple of days." I hand him another piece of plywood, and he adjusts it over the one last hole.

"We should've replaced this old roof when we remodeled the interior," I say, handing him another nail.

"Nah, this will work just fine."

"Have you started interviewing men to replace you when you become interim sheriff?"

"I met a ranch supervisor from Billings the other day when I was at the feed store. He came to town for the auction and was picking up a few supplies. I gave him a hand, loading his truck. His name was Hardin. We got to talking, and he'd like to work on a bigger cattle ranch. He said he'd be willing to move to Missoula, so I got his number and told him there might be a position for him in the near future if he'd send me his references."

"Did he send you his references?"

"Yeah, and so far, he looks like a great candidate."

"You'll be hard to replace, and we'll need someone trustworthy."

"Once we know for sure of his background, and if I'll be instated as sheriff, I'll set up a meeting at the ranch so you can interview him along with the rest of our family."

"I have no doubt, once the people of this town get to know you, you'll be elected sheriff.

We gather our tools and climb down the ladder. "How are things going with Greer?"

"Really great. She's loving being back at the elementary school substituting. She's been offered a job at the local community college teaching math next year."

"Good for her. Any repercussions from her father yet?"

"She said he keeps texting her and leaving her voicemails about financial issues."

"Not being able to sell his cattle was a financial hit, but with the money he's raking in from this community and the property he owns, I'm sure it was only a minor inconvenience."

"Word around town, according to Greer, is that the ranchers and the store owners have collectively come together after the petition was signed and are refusing to pay him his monthly tolls on their businesses."

"I'm glad to see they're taking some initiative on their own."

Knox comes trotting toward us on her horse. "Hey. Mercy says she's been trying to reach both of you by phone."

"We've been on the roof repairing it. Our phones are in the barn," I say.

"Mercy overheard at the market that Dustin bailed Lance out of jail this morning. Alden supposedly cut Lance off, and he's been bullying several of the ranchers into giving him the money they owe his father."

"Damn it." I slam the toolbox. "Why the heck would Dustin bail him out after almost costing him his life?"

"Probably for the simple fact that they are brothers," Chase states.

I march into the barn, grabbing my phone, and it rings in my hand with Blaise's number.

"Hey, man, I don't have time to..."

"I'm in the emergency room," he cuts me off.

"Why? What happened?" I ask, returning to Knox and Chase.

"The Alden brothers is what happened. I was coming out of the feed store, and they jumped me. I could've handled one of them, but not both."

"How badly are you beat up?" I grind my teeth in anger, putting him on speakerphone for Chase to hear.

"Lance cracked his cast into my side. I think my ribs are broken. My lip is busted, and I'll need a few stitches above my right eye that's swollen shut. Other than that, some bruises.

"I'm on my way," Chase barks, storming to his truck.

"I'm sorry that you've been drawn into this just by being my family."

"I don't blame you. They're just lucky I didn't have my gun on me, or they'd be the ones at the hospital having bullets removed."

"I'm going to head to the school to make sure there are no issues for Greer and Granger at dismissal. Let me know what the doctor says and if they admit you. If not, Chase will bring you home." I hang up, making a beeline for my Dodge.

The last bell of the day rings as I'm parking. School children clamor outside, either finding their parents to walk or ride their bikes home or in the car pick-up line. Granger comes out the door, talking with a little blond-haired girl wearing pigtails and pink cowgirl boots. Greer is holding the door open for students to exit. Moseying over to them, Greer displays a pretty smile when she sees me.

"Hey, cowboy. I thought Mercy was picking up Granger today?"

"She'll be here. I wanted to check on the two of you." I kiss her cheek.

Her smile fades when her brows draw together. "Why? Did something happen?"

I lean in and whisper in her ear. "Dustin bailed Lance out of jail this morning. They ganged up on Blaise, and he's landed in the emergency room."

Her mouth gapes with a gasp, and she covers it with her hand. "Is he going to be alright?"

"Possible broken ribs and stitches."

"I can't believe Dustin bailed him out after promising me he'd stay away from him."

"My guess is your father got to him."

"That doesn't make any sense. My dad would've bailed him out himself if he wanted Lance free."

"Then Lance convinced him."

"Once I'm done with my work, I'll go find him."

"I don't want you confronting either of them alone."

"They won't hurt me."

"I'm not willing to take that chance."

She runs her hand down my arm as if she's trying to reassure me. "They're a pain in the ass, but I'm their sister, and they won't harm me physically. You need to go see Blaise and make sure everyone else is secure. Don't worry about me. I'll be fine."

"No. If you go, I go. End of discussion," I bark.

Granger's friend gets into her parents' car, and

that's when he realizes I'm standing behind him. "What are you doing here, Daddy?" He looks up.

"Is that your new girlfriend?" I point at the car.

"Isn't Katie purty?" He's all smiles.

"She is." I laugh.

My phone rings. "It's Mercy," I say, stepping away to answer it.

"I have a flat tire, and I'm madder than a snake marrying a garden hose," she says in a huff.

"I'm here at the school. I'll grab Granger and come get you. Send me your coordinates on GPS."

"Is she okay?" Greer asks.

"Her tire is flat, and she's in a horn-tossing mood. I'll take Granger and go help her. Promise me you'll come straight to the ranch when you're done and call me when you're on your way." I don't wait for her to answer. There'll be hell to pay if I make Mercy wait one minute longer than she has to.

"This ain't just a flat. Your tire has been sliced," I say, squatting in front of it, running my fingers over the tread.

"I'm going to do some serious harm to the Alden brothers." She stomps her foot in the dirt. "I knew they were up to no good when I saw them coming out of the market."

"This isn't the only damage they've caused today. They beat up Blaise. I'm waiting for an update on him from Chase. He went to the ER, and I left to make sure my son and Greer were alright."

"Those two better give their hearts to Jesus because when I find them, their butts are mine," she rants, and my phone rings again.

"How is Blaise," I answer it.

"Two broken ribs and twelve stitches. They want to keep him overnight for observation, but he's refusing. Sheriff Grady showed up after the ER doctor called to file a report. He acted nonchalant about the ambush and said he'd arrest them, but I highly doubt he'll do anything."

"I don't blame Blaise for not wanting to stay, but tell him to chill for the night. There's no telling if they'll show up at our place tonight. I'll have one of our men guard his hospital room. Tell him I'll bring him supper. I need you back at the ranch to help Walker with the men."

"Will do, boss man," he says.

About the time I shove my phone in my pocket to get the jack from Mercy's car, the sheriff approaches and rolls his window down, stopping when he sees me. "Appears to me your family is having a bit of trouble today," he sneers with a gruff laugh.

"This is the handiwork of the Alden boys." I rest my forearms on his open window.

"You got any proof?" He lifts the corner of his lip.

"Wouldn't matter none to you if I did or not. You'll just keep protecting them."

"With that attitude, I'd let them beat the tar out of you too."

I stand tall, inhaling. "Have yourself a good day," I say.

"How's that girlfriend of yours?" he growls and speeds away when I lunge toward the cruiser.

"I swear I don't know if I can keep from killing him if he flexes his muscles about Greer again," I mumble low enough that Granger can't hear me, but Mercy does.

"He's going to have a lot of people wanting to take him out," she says, whispering.

I haul the spare tire out of her trunk and get to work on changing it. She crawls into my truck with Granger and turns the music up. I laugh when I see their heads bobbing and mouthing the words to a song.

CHAPTER TEN

GREER

I know River wanted me to come straight home, but my Bronco seems to have a mind of its own when it turns in the direction of my aunt's house. Mom's car is parked out front, along with Dustin's.

Not bothering to knock, I rush through the door in a tizzy. "What in the world were you thinking?" I holler.

Mom is sitting in a chair in the living room with my two brothers sitting on the couch with their dusty boots propped on the coffee table. "Why are you allowing him in this house?" I march to my mother, pointing at Lance.

"He's my son," she sniffs. "His father deserted him in jail."

"And you think by letting him in here, he's going to change his ways?" I yell. "Did he tell you the two of them beat up River's cousin, and he landed in the hospital?"

She glares at them. "No. You told me you were going to straighten out your life," she aims her words at Dustin.

"He told me if I didn't bail him out and go along with him, he'd tell all our secrets, and I'd be in the cell with him."

I can't keep my feet from barreling in front of Lance. "You are pure evil, just like our father. Dustin has a chance to change his ways, but it's clearly too late for you. You should be ashamed of yourself."

"Ain't no shame in my game," he says smugly, placing his boots on the floor.

"How do you think you're going to manage without our father behind your nonsense?" I cross my arms.

"Simple. The same way I convinced my brother here." He grabs Dustin firmly on the back of his neck. "You may think me stupid, but I have records, just like you, of every order dear old dad has given me. I recorded the night he told me to kill the rancher in case he ever decided to turn on me. When I share it with him, he'll change his mind."

"Fine. Do whatever you want with him, but leave Dustin and our mother out of it. Let them have a chance at a good life."

He stands, sneering down at me with his lip curled. "Like you with the Methany boy? I wouldn't get too comfortable believing in happily ever after. He ain't no prince, and you surely are no Sleeping Beauty," he spats through his teeth, then jerks me by the hair. "Don't think because we're kin, I won't take you out if you get in my way," he snarls. It burrows under his skin like a gopher in a garden when I don't flinch. "You chose the wrong team!" He breathes fire.

"Team! We're supposed to be family! Not a team to gang up on other people. You have no idea what it's like to truly be a family and be loved by either parent!" I snap.

"That's enough!" Our mother rises. "I may not have been the perfect parent, but I do love each of you."

"Don't go listening to her crap. She has no idea either!" Lance lets go of me. "She just thinks she's better than us, always has. Once I get my hands on our father's fortune, you'll see who the better person is." His greed comes awful heavy, like a wet wool blanket suffocating, snuffing out his light.

"You think money makes you better than anyone

else?" I snort. "It's the heart of a man that makes him." I turn up my nose.

He laughs, then slaps me hard across the face. My head jolts to the side from the force of it, and I hold my cheek. "You'll learn to respect me," he jeers.

"You're not a man. You're a monster, and I'll never respect the likes of you!" I say with a calmness I didn't know I had.

"Leave her alone." Dustin steps between us when Lance rears back his hand to strike me again. "She's right. I don't want to be like you or our father. Tell the authorities whatever you need to about me. I'm willing to go to jail if it derails you from the path you're on." He lengthens his spine, jutting his chin.

Lance growls in pure frustration, snatching his hat before he hoofs it out the front door, punishing it with a slam.

Dustin angles my face so he can look at it. "I'm so sorry. I'll go turn myself in for what I did to River's cousin."

"It won't do any good. The sheriff will look the other way." I turn to my mother. "I hate what this family has become. You say you want things to be different, then stay clear of Lance. He ain't no better than Daddy, maybe worse."

"Now that I've seen it with my own two eyes, I

have no doubt about what you're saying." My mother lays her palm on the side of my face. "I'm sorry. I won't make the same mistake again."

"Perhaps it's not safe for the two of you to be here."

"I'll make arrangements for us to go stay with my brother in Nevada. He'll take us in until I can get on my feet. I filed for a divorce, but it's going to be a long battle. In the meantime, I'll get a job, and maybe Dustin can go to college where he belongs, far away from his brother's influence." She twists her face toward him.

"I'd like that." He smiles a genuine smile that I've not seen since he was a little boy.

"Come with us," she says.

"I'm not going anywhere. I belong with River and Granger. They make me happy and bring so much joy to my life. I'm not about to leave them because of my father. It's taken me a lifetime to feel what I feel for River and know that he loves me the same."

"But it's not safe here. He'll have River killed to get what he wants."

"River is smarter than Daddy. He'll stop him before he harms another person." I place both my hands on her shoulders. "How quickly do you think you can leave?"

"We can be gone by this evening," she says.

"Good. Don't tell anyone where you are going, and get rid of your phones. Text me your new numbers."

She drags me in for a long, hard hug as if she may never see me again. "I love you, my daughter."

"I love you, too, Mom. Now hurry and pack," I say, stepping back, staring at Dustin. "You can be a good man. I just know it."

"I'm going to make you proud of me, you'll see." I hug him, then fly out the door.

Before I can get in my Bronco, the sheriff blocks the driveway directly behind me. "Well, if it isn't Greer Alden," he says, leaning out the window. "Where do you think you're going in an all-fire hurry?"

"It's none of your business," I snarl.

"Seems with you going through with your petition to have me ousted, everything you do is my business."

"How do you figure?" I plod toward him.

"You're so naïve." His nose wrinkles as if he caught a whiff of a raccoon long dead. His laughter dumps hot coals into the pit of my belly, tying it in knots strong enough to hold back even the wildest of horses. "Your father has promised me if I were ever to be thrown out of my position in this town, you'd be at my disposal. Whether my hankering for you is love or hate, I guess you'll find out in due time. You'll regret being the one instigating this town to have me removed. You have yourself a mighty fine rest of your day." He salutes me with two fingers and slowly drives off.

My entire body shivers as I blink rapidly, trying to press down the fear growing inside of me. That's what they both want, for me to be afraid. "I will not back down!" I yell between my hands down the road.

I race back to the ranch, knowing River will be worried about me if I'm late. He's leaning on the front porch post, waiting for me when I pull up. Peering in the mirror on the visor, my skin is still pink, where Lance slapped me. Inhaling, I lower my chin and get out, dragging my feet.

"Where've you been? I was worried." He glances at his watch.

"I had an errand to run," I say, stopping on the bottom step.

He strides three steps and lifts my chin, and his lips flatten, and his expression tightens. "Who did this to you?"

"I'm alright," I try to ease his anger.

"That's not what I asked you," he says calmly, but his jaw flexes.

"Lance." I blow out my cheeks.

He grows silent, disengaging from the conversation, and I know he's stewing.

"I handled it. My mother and Dustin are leaving town tonight. This thing between my father and brother is going to implode on itself."

He runs his hand down my arm. "Then why are you shivering?"

"Grady stopped by my aunt's house as I was leaving. He said if he's thrown out of office, I'm his to do what he wants to, a promise made by my father."

He grasps me to his chest. "He'll never get his hands on you. You're done working, and you'll not leave the ranch."

I wrench out of his arms. "I won't be held a prisoner because they think I'm afraid."

"You are afraid, or you wouldn't be shaking like a leaf."

"The point is, you can't keep me locked up. I know you mean well, but I won't be controlled by anyone, not even you." I stare into his eyes, letting him know I'm serious.

"I'm not trying to contain you. My only intention is to keep you safe."

"And I appreciate your protectiveness, but not by ordering me to give up my day-to-day life."

"Fine, but I'll have one of my men outside the school at all times. It's not only for your protection, but Granger's as well."

"That I'll concede to," I say, wrapping my arms around his waist.

"I would've ripped him apart if I saw him slap you," he says, with an ache in his voice.

"How is Blaise?" I peer up at him.

"He'll stay the night in the hospital for observation and be home tomorrow."

"I'm so sorry that this was at the hands of my brothers. Dustin was willing to go to the authorities and admit what he'd done. I didn't feel like it would do any good. He's as much a victim of my brother and father as anyone else in this town, including myself."

"It's all fixing to end. I promise."

"I hope so and that it doesn't cost anyone their life in the process." I step up on my tiptoes and kiss him softly. "Will you hold me?" I whisper against his lips.

"You never have to ask." He takes my hand, leading me to our bedroom.

CHAPTER ELEVEN
RIVER

Five days later...

"HAVE you heard the local headlines this morning?" Blaise pushes pause on the television set in the living room.

"I don't tend to watch the news on Saturday morning," I grumble, tired from being up all night with a pregnant heifer who needed assistance to deliver her calf.

"The coffee is fresh," Mercy says, taking down a mug from the cabinet for me. "You're going to need it." She fills the cup, then hands it to me as I follow her into the living room.

"You may want to sit," Blaise states, aiming the remote at the television.

I listen as the local newscaster talks about the petition that was filed against the sheriff and that he was removed from his position today, but not without protest. He turned in his badge, but only one of his weapons. The other was reported as missing by Grady. There's an interview with him, ranting about how people will pay for the injustice done to him. Alden was behind him and took the microphone, saying there had been a grave mistake and he planned on righting the wrong done to Sheriff Grady and that it would only be temporary. He'd be back in charge. Blaise pauses the news.

"He's doing everything he can to keep Grady in his position to cover his ass," Chase says, marching down the stairs wearing a slick new pair of jeans, a white button-down, with a new white Stetson. "The mayor called and wants me at the station. He's going to announce me as interim sheriff of Missoula."

"That's the best news I've heard in a long time." I get up and shake his hand.

"Wait, there's more." Blaise hits play.

"*Lance Alden has harpooned his father with accusa-*

tions, along with his sister, Greer Alden. If these allegations prove to be legitimate, whoever is elected sheriff will have to detain the lifetime resident of Missoula."

"Where is Greer?" I ask, looking around the room.

"I thought she was upstairs with you," Mercy says.

"Her Bronco is parked out front." Blaise points.

I run up the stairs to check Granger's room and our bathroom in case I missed her. "Greer!" I holler. Once I'm sure she's not upstairs, I trot back to the living room. "She's not in the house," I say, skating out the door, down the porch steps, at a fast pace to the barn. "Greer!" I yell again.

"She took Granger on an early ride. What's got your tail feathers all ruffled?" Knox asks as her horse nuzzles her pockets to make sure all the carrots are gone, then he rests his chin on her shoulder.

"Do you know where they were riding to?"

"Granger wanted to go down by the river. I told Greer the best spot was on the east side after Tumble butte."

"I need your horse." I grab a saddle from its mount, tossing it on the horse and strapping it underneath him.

"What's going on?"

"Grady has been removed from office, and Lance is running his mouth about Greer. I need to make sure neither one of them can get to her." Taking the horse by the reins, I walk him out of the stable, step on the stirrup, swing my leg over, and take off almost in a full gallop to the east side of the property. I bounce hard on the leather saddle as I have him in full stride past the corrals, over the first set of hills, through a wooded area, and down to the river. I make it to the butte and shield my eyes from the early morning rays of the sun. My heart stops when I look out into a field and see two horses with no one on them.

I make a clicking noise with my tongue and dig my heels into the horse. He takes off down the butte to the grassy area. "Greer!" I yell her name for the third time today.

Two heads pop up from the tall grass. "Over here." She laughs, chasing Granger.

I take a few slow, deep breaths to calm myself. "She's okay," I say to myself.

"Daddy! We saw a snake being carried away by a hawk." Granger runs to me when I dismount my horse.

"What are you doing out here so early?" I hold his hand, marching through the tall grass where

Greer has lain back with her hands weaved behind her head.

"I had a bad dream, and Greer decided we'd chase it away by riding the horses," he says, grinning at me.

"I'm sorry. I didn't mean to worry you. I knew you'd been up all night, and when I heard him cry out, I thought I'd see if I could help." She sits, covering her brow with her hand to look at me.

I sit on the grass next to her.

"Are you angry?" she asks.

"No. I was just worried when I couldn't find you."

Granger jots a few feet out, trying to catch a yellow and black butterfly.

"You look shaken. What's wrong?" She sits, weaving her hand with mine.

"The sheriff has been removed from office."

"That's great news." She smiles, then it turns into a frown. "There's something you're not saying, isn't there?"

"Lance has made some accusations about you being part of what your father has done to this town."

"That isn't a surprise to me. I told you I'd be willing to take some heat."

"You did. I just don't like it."

"I don't either, but it's a consequence I'll pay for turning a blind eye for him."

I wrap my arm around her shoulder. "Thanks for taking care of Granger. He's not had a nightmare in several weeks. I wonder what brought it on?"

"He's a very intuitive little boy. I'm sure the stress of the situation has been apparent to him, and it's misplaced in his dreams."

"You're so good with him."

"I love him as much as I love you. He makes it easy." She places a sweet kiss on my lips. "Thank you for sharing him with me."

I laugh. "I don't think I had a choice. Some days, I think he likes you more than me."

"Don't be silly. He adores you." She lays her head on my shoulder. "What do you think is going to happen next?"

"Chase will be sheriff, and he'll know what to do to get you out of this mess. In the meantime, please don't go running off without telling me. I was terrified one of them had gotten to you. My heart fell plum to my feet."

"I'll be a little more vocal next time. Everyone was still sleeping except for Knox. Does she ever sleep?" She cocks her head to the side.

"She's never been one to sleep much. It used to

drive Aunt Ellie insane. It had gotten so bad, she'd lock the doors at night and make sure there wasn't anything Knox could get into and go to bed. She said she'd find her the next morning, lying face down on the cold tile floor, with her princess panties on and a pair of click-clack shoes."

I giggle.

"That's when she was a teenager."

Greer howls. "Surely you're kidding."

"I am, but she didn't sleep much then either." I chuckle at her getting so tickled. I love laughing with her. She's been so happy since she moved in with us. Mercy and Knox both enjoy having her around.

"I didn't ask how the heifer did?"

"It was a close call, but she and the calf are doing fine. She'll need a little extra attention for a few days, but that's all."

"I caught it!" Granger clasps his hands together, stumbling over to us. He opens his hands to show us, but the butterfly flies away. "Darn it," he shouts.

"Come here." I tap the dirt beside me for him to sit. "What was your dream about?" I ask him.

"I kept seeing a man, but I couldn't see his face. He was in my room and said he'd be taking me away. I cried and screamed for you, but you didn't come."

"Ah, buddy. You know it wasn't real, right? I'd always come for you if you needed me."

"That's what Greer said." He looks over me at her.

"She's a smart lady." I ruffle his hair. "We should get back to the house. You've got eggs to gather from the henhouse, and I have to check on the new calf." I get up, extending my hand to Greer to pull her off the ground. "Thanks again for taking such good care of my son. I'm sorry I was upset with you."

"No need to apologize. You had good reason to be scared," she whispers out of earshot of Granger.

We all mount our horses and casually ride back to the stable, enjoying the scenery along the way.

"I see you found them," Knox says, leading her horse into the barn after I dismount.

"After I check on the calf, I want to run to town to support Chase. Do you want to come with me?" I ask Greer.

She looks at Granger, then at Knox.

"Don't worry. He and I can hang out today after he does his chores," Knox says.

"Alright then. I'd love to be there for Chase." She places her hand in the crook of my arm.

"You mind your aunt Knox while I'm gone. Don't

leave her side unless you're with one of your other aunts or uncles." I wave a finger at Granger.

"I know, I know." He rolls his eyes.

"I'd like to get out of these clothes first, so I don't stink like a smelly horse." Greer sniffs her armpit.

"That's fine. I'm starving. I'll grab something to eat while you get cleaned up." We walk hand in hand back to the house. The heavenly scent of bacon and biscuits fill the entire downstairs. I snag two slices of bacon when Mercy isn't looking.

"Are you hungry?" She turns as I'm chomping the bacon. "I guess that's a yes." She points the metal tongs at me.

"Starved. I missed dinner last night and got caught up in things this morning. I never even drank the coffee you made me."

"It's sitting right where you left it. You can heat it up in the microwave."

I pick it up and do just that while she piles a biscuit with an egg on a napkin, handing it to me. "I'm assuming you're going to town."

"Yes, and Greer is coming with me. Knox volunteered to entertain Granger while I'm gone."

"Walker's already done a walkthrough on the property. After the news this morning, he gathered the men, and he looks like he's fit for battle. He's got two pistols, a rifle, and a knife stuck in his boot."

"Where is he?"

"In the rocker on the front porch." She peers out the kitchen window.

I mosey out to him. "You being prepared is a good thing, but perhaps you could be a little reserved with Granger running about. It might scare him."

"He's already asked me if I'd take him shooting," he says with a grin.

"I hope you told him no." I take a seat.

"Uncle Boone had you handling a BB gun when you were his age. Every one of us kids knew how to handle a shotgun by the time we were twelve."

"Our life differed greatly from Granger's."

"How so?" He tilts his head to the side.

"He's had trauma in his life we never had at his age. I want him to learn to choose his words before I ever let him shoot any kind of gun."

"I told him he had to clear it with you first. I'd never assume to teach him something like that without your permission."

"Thank you," I say, standing when Greer pops out onto the porch.

"Mercy packed these for you and put your coffee

in a to-go cup. She's betting it's cold before you drink it."

"She's probably right. You ready to go?"

She nods.

"Keep watch," I say, following Greer to the Dodge.

She slides in the middle, opening the food wrapped in napkins. I get crumbs all over my plaid shirt and the truck from scarfing it down. I end up tossing the coffee out of the truck window because it's cold as ice.

When we make it to town, there's a crowd at the station door. I escort Greer with my hand on her lower back.

"Is it true? Are we finally rid of Grady?" one townsperson asks.

"What I want to know is how long did you know your father has been stealing money from us?" a rancher asks, pointing at Greer.

I hustle her inside before the crowd grows angry. Chase is inside with the mayor, who's speaking in front of a camera, announcing Chase as Grady's temporary replacement. Also stating that if Alden steps out of line to call the phone number on the screen. Any and all reports would be taken seriously and acted upon by Sheriff Chase Calhoun.

CHAPTER TWELVE

GREER

Chase stands in front of the podium with his hands braced on either side. "I willingly accept the temporary position of Sheriff of Missoula. My first order of business will be to investigate the petition filed by the people of this town that has now turned into a criminal charge against Grady." He stops briefly, gazing down, and then flattens his lips when he lifts his head, looking at me. "I would be derelict in my duties if I ignored the accusations against Greer Alden."

River inhales sharply and puffs out his chest. I squeeze his hand. "It's okay," I whisper. "He's doing his job."

"Rumor has it she's moved into your home," a man yells.

"I can assure you, my relationship with Ms. Alden will not interfere with my duties." Chase clears his throat.

Letting loose of River's hand, I step up to Chase. "May I speak?" I ask.

He takes one large step backward, and I walk up to the microphone. My lip quivers as I address the townspeople. "I owe each and every one of you an apology for the way my father has treated you and for me keeping his secrets for far too long. I could make an excuse for myself, but I won't. I will pay restitution for my part. Most of you have known me all my life. Missoula has always been my home, and I love the way the town used to be. My wish is that with Sheriff Grady out of office and my family losing the control they've had over so many of you, we'll get back to the friendly, happy town we once were. I'm sorry that I wasn't strong enough until now to fight my father and brothers." My gaze cuts to River, knowing he's the reason I found my strength.

Several of the ranchers clap. "You're the reason we've come this far in cleaning up this town. If it weren't for you gathering us together to have Grady removed, we'd still be paying your father his bribe money every month. I'd say you've done enough and paid your price." Old man Smith stands in front of the ranchers, helping me out.

"Yeah, leave Greer alone. She's slipped me money any time I was short to keep her father from coming after me," a rancher hollers.

"Me too," another one says.

"She paid my mortgage when she got wind I was going to go to her father for help, even though I knew it would cost me. When I was able to get back on my feet, I tried to repay her, and she refused to take a dime from me," Tom, who has lived two roads down from me my entire life, declares.

Tears fill my eyes with gratitude.

"When my land was being foreclosed on, she went to the bank and borrowed money before her father took it for pennies on the dollar. Alden had no idea how I came up with the money at the last minute. She saved my ranch and my family from being evicted. Whatever she hid for her father, she's more than made up for," Mr. Baker yells between his hands.

Chase touches my shoulder, and I move back as he takes over. "Then, if the town is satisfied, there will be no charge brought against her. I will, however, have her turn over any information regarding the illegal activities of her father." I nod and wipe away my tears, and join River off to the side.

He kisses my temple. "You never shared any of those stories with me. I'm so proud of you."

To hear those words that have never been spoken to me brings up bubbling sobs. I cry on his chest. "Thank you," I rasp.

Each rancher and storeowner shakes my hand before they leave. Chase waits until everyone is gone before he speaks to me. "I thought there was going to be a lynching for a bit. Turns out you're a remarkable, caring woman. You helped this town even when keeping your father's secrets. I'm glad I didn't have to take you into custody."

"Me too," River chimes in.

"You know the best part of all of those stories?" I grin.

"What?" River asks.

"It was all done with my father's money, and he has no idea. I used what he'd stolen from them without a trace."

"Damn, woman. I love you more and more by the minute." River embraces me, and Chase claps me on the back. "Let's get you out of here." River grips my hand and leads the way out the front door, where the townspeople are still lingering, chatting with one another.

"You aren't getting off that easily," someone growls and pushes his way through, knocking a lady down.

"Lance!" I gasp as he aims a gun at me.

"If I'm going down for our father's crimes, so are you!"

River protectively shoves me behind him. Chase wheels a gun from his holster. "Put the gun down. You don't want to do this," he grits between his teeth.

"I don't care what these people say. You're as guilty as he is. You've made them all think I'm the bad guy when in fact, you've always been our father's right-hand man!" he yells, trying to convince the people to believe him.

I move from around River. "He will not hurt me. It's all show. These people know what you've done to them. You saying it ain't so doesn't change the fact that you've bullied every one of them in the name of the Alden family, which I'm ashamed of. You have a chance to do the right thing. Turn yourself in and tell Sheriff Calhoun everything you know about our father."

"She's a liar!" he seethes, with his finger inching toward the trigger. "I was acting on her orders, not my father's."

"What did he promise you to make me look guilty?" I narrow my eyes.

"Nothing. Not a damn thing," he denies with his gaze cutting at the ranchers around him. "With the two of you behind bars, I'll be the sole owner of Alden Enterprises. I'll make sure there is restitution to each of you they stole from," he spats.

"He's the liar. You've shown up at my house in the middle of the night and aimed a gun at my wife, swearing to kill her if I didn't give you cash," Mr. Baker barks.

Lance swings the gun toward him, and a shot is fired. Lance blinks a few times and looks down at the blood pooling on his shirt. The gun falls to the ground, and he drops to his knees. He looks over his shoulder to see Chase with the smoking gun.

I run over to him, easing him to the ground with his head in my lap. His eyes glaze over as he stares up at me. "I'm sorry, sis," he says, with blood spewing from his lips. "Take him down," he gurgles, closing his eyes and taking his last breath.

"I'm sorry I couldn't get you from his clutches," I cry, rocking back and forth.

One by one, the crowd leaves as the sound of an ambulance rolls toward us, stopping in the parking lot.

River squats next to me, splaying his hand on my neck. "He's gone, baby."

I sniff, getting to my feet. "I know he was awful, but he was still my brother."

"I know." He holds me.

He doesn't let go until the paramedics have carried Lance off in a body bag. I hear Chase's deep voice over my shoulder. "I didn't want to kill him," he says solemnly.

I lick my lips and wipe my nose with the back of my hand, and turn to face him. "You did your job. He would've killed Mr. Baker with a single shot. I'm not angry with you, just sad that Lance was so bitter and greedy. It cost him his life."

Chase takes both my hands in his. "Is there anything I can do for you?"

"Make my father pay for what he's done. I'll give you every piece of evidence I have against him."

"He will pay for his crimes," he says.

"Let me take you home." River has his hands on my waist.

I nod, and he shuffles me to his truck. The road home seems much longer as I stare out the window, trying to recall any of the good times I shared with my brother growing up. He used to be a sweet thing. At what point did he change? What abuse did he receive at the hands of our father? He's the one that should be held accountable for his own son's death. Lance turned into what my father wanted him to be and forgot who he was.

As we turn onto the dirt road to the ranch, I take my phone out of my purse. "My mother needs to hear the story from me. Not some stranger on the television or whatever perversion of the story my father may give her."

River parks on the side of the dirt road before we make it to the ranch sign. He unbuckles and scoots next to me, holding me as I make the call to tell my mother her son is dead and the actual facts of how it happened.

I softly shed my last tears for Lance on River's shoulder. They are more for my mother's broken heart than anything else. Once I'm all cried out, without a word, he moves back to the driver's seat and starts the truck, pulling into the ranch.

Mercy, Knox, Blaise, and Walker are all sitting on the porch, waiting for us. As soon as I get out, Mercy runs into my arms. "I'm so sorry," she says, followed by the same words coming from the rest of them.

"You're truly my family. Every one of you had reason to loathe my brother, yet you're consoling me for his loss."

"What your brother did had nothing to do with you. We'll share your grief. That's what family is for," Knox says with watery eyes.

"We'll help you with anything you need," Walker says.

"Thank you. I appreciate each of you. Right now, I think I'd just like a hot shower and to lie down for a bit."

We all walk into the house, and River walks with his hand on my back up the stairs. He turns on the hot shower while I stare into the mirror, mascara streaked down my cheeks.

"Hey," he says, wrapping his arms around me. "You alright?"

"I will be," I say, nodding.

"Let me help you," he says, undressing me like a child. He takes my hand, putting me into the shower. "I'll be in the bedroom if you need anything."

I don't let go of this hand when he tries to leave. "Stay with me," I say faintly. He doesn't bother undressing as he steps into the shower with me. His clothes drench, soaking him to the skin as he wraps his arms tightly around me, swaying as if there is music playing. He hums a tune in my ear, and I melt into his arms, feeling every ounce of his love for me. Slowly, I strip him of his clothes, letting them fall to the tile floor, holding him skin to skin. I want to show him the same love he's giving me. My finger-nails graze his abs as I get on my knees. Gazing up at him, I blink back the spray of the water. "Let me love you," I say, licking my lips. He braces his hands on the wall behind me and lowers his head, watching me wrap my mouth around his cock, drawing him in. He hisses but doesn't take his lustful eyes off mine.

He lowers his hand, touching my face with the back of his hand. "I love you."

His words set me on fire. I cradle his balls in my hand and massage them with every stroke of my tongue down his growing cock. My insides burn for him to be inside me, but I want this to be all about him. I continue with my slow, ardent torture of him as he moans. I know he's getting close when his back stiffens. He places his hand in my hair and slightly tugs as he throbs in my mouth. I don't back off. I suck him in and out as his salty warmth fills my tongue, lapping him up. When he's done, I brace my hands on his thighs, get off the shower floor, and kiss my way up his stomach to his chest. He draws my face to his, ravaging my lips, swallowing me whole.

"I love you too," I finally respond with words.

CHAPTER THIRTEEN

RIVER

"Daddy, what happens when you die?" Granger asks me as I tuck him into bed. He knows we buried Greer's brother today.

"Well, there's no simple answer. If you believe in God, your soul goes to heaven."

"What's a soul?"

I place my hand on his chest. "It's what's inside of you. The heart of who you are."

"Is my mommy in heaven?" He blinks.

"Yes. Your mommy was such a good, loving woman."

"Sometimes I think I miss her, but I don't remember her at all."

"That's because you were still a baby. Our minds

don't go back that far." He rolls to his side, folding his hands under his cheek. "Your mother loved you every bit as much as I do."

"And Greer?" he asks.

"And Greer." I brush the hair from his forehead. "Get some sleep." He closes his eyes. Easing off the bed, I turn off the light and leave his door cracked open.

Greer is standing in the hallway, peeking into his room. "How is he?"

I take her hand, drawing her into the bedroom. "He asked me what happens when you die."

"He's such a sweet kid. I wish he'd never had to experience death at such a young age."

"He doesn't recall his mother, and I think that bothers him. I wish his little mind would forget the trauma."

"He will one day, and he'll grow up with great memories to replace the bad ones." She grabs her purse.

"Where are you going?" I ask.

"I want to spend some time with my mother and Dustin before they leave town again. They're staying at a hotel in town and leaving first thing in the morning. Dustin is taking Lance's death pretty hard."

"I'm sure he is. I'll get my keys and drive you."

She runs her hand down my arm. "I'd like to spend time with them alone if that's okay."

"I can stay in the truck."

"I'm going to stay the night. You should be here in case Granger has a nightmare."

"What about your father? He's not been seen since Lance was killed."

"I thought he'd show up at the funeral today."

"He knows Chase has a warrant out for his arrest. He might go looking for your mother."

"I know you're worried, but I need to do this alone, please," she pleads with me.

"Alright, but keep your phone on you and carry the gun I bought you."

"I will," she says, kissing me sweetly.

I squeeze her ass. "I'll miss you being in my bed and underneath me."

"Or on top of you." She giggles.

"That too." I smile.

"I'll be back once I drop them off at the airport in the morning. I promise." I walk her downstairs and make sure she's safely in her Bronco. "I love you," she mouths through the window.

"I love you too." I wave, watching her back out of

the driveway, and I wait until I can no longer see her tail lights driving down the dirt road.

Walker is in the kitchen pouring a glass of water when I ease into the house. "How is Greer holding up?"

"She's remarkably good."

Chase enters through the screen door, kicking the dirt from his boots. "Was that Greer driving off?" he asks.

"She's going to stay with her mother and brother tonight."

"She's a damn strong woman," he states.

He's shared with me how bad he feels about killing her brother. "She has no ill will toward you," I say, knowing he's struggling. "She knows what he was capable of, and she's grateful you stopped him. She'd rather have seen him dead than kill an innocent man."

"She told you as much?"

"She did, so quit beating yourself up for doing your job."

He hangs his hat on a hook by the back door. "Now if I could only locate Alden."

"He'll show his face, eventually. I'm sure he and Grady are held up together somewhere plotting and planning their revenge."

"I plan on stopping them before they get it," he says.

A blood-curdling scream has me taking the stairs three at a time. I flip on the overhead light as I swing open Granger's door. He's in the middle of a night terror, standing in the center of his bed swinging his arms frantically, screaming to get away from him.

I gingerly meander toward him as Walker and Chase watch from the hallway. "Hey, I say, keeping my voice low. "It's okay. It's a dream."

With his eyes wide open, and a high-pitched wail, he punches his fists upward. "Let me go!"

"Granger," I call his name louder. "It's Daddy. You're safe, son."

He drops his hands freely to his sides and closes his eyes. His pajama bottoms stick to him as he wets himself.

Gently, I touch his arm. "It's alright. It's just a dream," I say.

His eyes peek open. "Daddy," he says.

"Yes." I full-on put my hand on his shoulder.

He looks down at his pajamas. "I'm sorry," he cries.

"It's alright. No harm done." He crawls into my arms, wrapping his legs around me, wet pajamas and all. I don't let it faze me. "I've got you. Nothing bad is going to happen to you."

"He tried to take me away from you," he says, choking on his words.

"Who? Who tried to take you, son?"

"That man that keeps showing up in my dreams." His arms squeeze my neck as I walk him down the hall to the bathroom. Walker grabs a clean pair of pajamas from his dresser, and Chase pulls the sheets off the bed.

"He isn't real. Your mind has made him up."

"Why does it do that?" He leans back to look me in the eye.

"I don't know. It's something we'll have to ask the therapist."

"I thought I was done with him." He pouts.

"It wouldn't hurt to meet with him a few more times." I run the water in the tub.

"Why can't I just be normal, Daddy?"

"You are, Son. Anyone that's been through what you have would be in the same boat."

"Do you have nightmares?"

"Right after your mother died, I did. Not so much anymore. Yours have gotten to be less frequent. Given time, you won't have them anymore." He climbs into the tub. I pick up a washcloth, squirt soap on it, and lather him up. "How about after you're all cleaned up, you sleep in my bed tonight?"

"With you and Greer?" He tilts his head.

"She's gone for the night."

"You didn't make her mad, did you?" His eyes roll toward the sky.

"No." I chuckle. "She's spending the night with her mom."

"Good. Because I'd hate for her to leave us."

"Me, too, kiddo."

"You should ask her to marry you. I want her to be my mommy."

"We're still getting to know one another, and I'm not ready for marriage."

"What more do you need to know? You love her, and she loves you." His lips turn into a smirk.

"The kid has a point," Walker says from the doorway.

"Don't the two of you go ganging up on me," I snark.

"Three." Chase steps into the bathroom. "You'd be a fool not to marry her."

"The offer still stands. If you don't want her, I'll gladly step in your shoes." Walker laughs.

I take a towel from a drawer, holding it up for Granger to get out. "I think it's time for a lot of people to go to bed and mind their own damn business," I jeer.

"What's going on in here? Did I miss a party or something?" Knox struts between Chase and Walker.

"Our little nephew here was just advising River he should ask Greer to marry him, and we concur." Walker folds his arms over his chest.

"He should ask her while he's using his cattle prod. She'd surely say yes then." Knox elbows Chase in the gut, laughing.

"Cattle prod?" Granger wrinkles his nose. "What do the cattle prods have to do with Greer?"

"Never mind." I grit my teeth at Knox while holding in a chuckle.

The three of them part as I walk Granger to my room.

"Sleep on the idea, why don't ya?" Walker says.

"Not on the cattle prod, the idea of marriage," Knox hoots, then disappears into her room.

Chase stands in the doorway and shrugs, grinning.

I shut the door in his face. Granger crawls into Greer's side and opens his mouth as if he's going to add his two cents. "Not another word, or you'll find yourself sleeping on the floor," I grunt, change clothes, and get under the sheets. He zips his mouth closed with his fingers. "Smart man," I mutter before turning out the light.

I wake up in the morning with Granger twisted around me, lying crossways on the bed. Glancing at the clock, it's already seven thirty. I'm usually up by six working on the ranch.

"Hey." I shake his leg. "It's time to get up."

He groggily lifts his head with his hair standing straight up on one side and drool running from the corner of his mouth. "Huh," he moans.

"It's late. You should be in school, and you didn't take care of Rosie."

He jumps out of bed, bolting out of the room.

I move to the edge of the bed, sit, and stretch my arms out wide, yawning. Picking up my cell phone, I see a text from Greer.

I HOPE you had sweet dreams of me. I'm off to the airport with my mother and brother, and then I'm substitute teaching. I'll catch you after work. The text is followed by three heart emojis.

. . .

After I slip into my clothes, I make my way downstairs. Knox and Mercy are in their usual morning spots at the bar, laughing.

"What's so funny?" I ask, taking a pitcher of freshly squeezed orange juice out of the fridge.

"I heard there was an intervention last night brought on by your eight-year-old," Mercy snorts.

"Is that what we're calling it? I was thinking more like an ambush." I chuckle with an eye cocked at Knox.

"You really should think about marrying that girl. If she's willing to put up with all the crap around here and let you"—she turns her chin toward Knox—"how did you put it?"

"Shampooing the Wookie," she says in all seriousness, and orange juice spews across the room when I can't hold back my laughter.

"That was it. I would've messed it all up by saying cookie or something similar." Mercy snaps her fingers.

"Please don't make me explain what a Wookie is to my son," I roar.

"I'm just glad you know," Knox mutters from the corner of her mouth.

"You ladies enjoy your day. I'll grab something to eat on the way to Granger's school." I put my glass in the sink and go find my son to move him toward getting ready for school.

When I pull up in the drop-off line, Greer's dress is swishing as she briskly walks across the school-yard. I honk my horn, and she changes direction. She smiles, seeing Granger. Rolling down my window, she pokes her head inside.

"Hey, cowboy," she beams.

"Thanks for the text message this morning, letting me know you were okay. I missed you."

The late bell blares, and she looks at her watch.

"I gotta go. You can tell me all about your evening when I get home." She blows me a kiss.

I smile from ear to ear, watching her hips sway across the schoolyard. "Why don't I ask her to marry me?" I ask myself, shoving the gear into drive. She's a good woman that loves me for me and adores my son. I'd be a fool not to make her my wife.

CHAPTER FOURTEEN

RIVER

"Are you sure I should be doing this with Alden's whereabouts still unknown?" I stand back and watch as Mercy packs the last of Greer's clothes for my surprise weekend getaway.

"Chase assured me he has things handled. Knox and I will meet our parents in Utah so they can camp with Granger. Us girls will be horseback riding in the mountains while they keep him busy. You'll have no one to fret over while you're gone." She zips the suitcase. "Try to enjoy yourself and remember why you're going." She playfully swats me on the cheek. "Did you pack the ring?"

I take it out of the small box I stuffed in my backpack. "Do you think she'll like the fact that it was Grandma Amelia's?"

"She'll love it. I'm totally jealous." She slips the round one-carat diamond perched on a silver band onto her ring finger, holding it in the air, admiring it. "You're so lucky Grandpa passed this beauty on to your mother."

"When I called her the other day telling her I wanted to ask Greer to marry me, she shipped it overnight. I had no idea she even had it. She never offered it to me when I proposed to Paige."

"That's because she knew Paige was never going to marry you."

"Everyone else knew but me." I frown.

"You should be thankful. If it weren't for her, you'd never have left Salt Lick and found Greer. Paige gave you a son and a wonderful woman."

"When you say it like that, I guess you're right. It was worth all the trouble and heartache I went through to find her and to raise Granger."

She takes off the ring, slipping it back into the box. "When the two of you come back, we'll have to celebrate. There's a fancy new restaurant that just opened in town."

"Thanks for packing her things. I did not know

what she'd want to bring. For me, a pair of blue jeans and a couple of shirts would do."

"Please tell me you packed a pair of shorts?" She sprawls her hand on her hip.

I turn around, open a drawer and take out a pair of shorts, stuffing them in my bag. "Thanks for reminding me."

"And something other than a pair of boots," she adds.

"I own nothing other than boots. I'll have to purchase something there."

"She has no idea what she's in for, does she?" She laughs.

"Not a clue." I drag the suitcase off the bed and carry it to my truck. "Do you need anything else for Granger?"

"If I do, we'll get it in Utah. Stop worrying. He'll be in excellent hands."

"I'll see you when we get back. Have fun, and you and Knox stay out of trouble." I kiss her cheek.

The sky is bluer than blue on the drive to the school. I park in the employee parking lot, waiting for Greer to get done with the pickup line. She walks out the back with another teacher, laughing about something. She's so into the conversation she doesn't see me parked in a row behind her. I lay on the horn as she unlocks her Bronco. She jumps about a foot off the ground, holding her hand over her chest.

"You scared the bejesus out of me," she says, stomping over to the truck.

I slide out and dip in for a quick kiss. "Get in. I'm taking you somewhere." I shuffle her to the passenger side before she can argue with me.

"Where are we going?" she asks when I'm behind the wheel.

"It's a surprise."

"I'm not much on surprises," she says, buckling her seat belt. She peers over her shoulder at the suitcases in the back seat. "Seriously, where are you taking me?"

"You'll find out soon enough." I grin, pulling out onto the main road.

"Did you pack clothes for me? Because if you did, I'm scared." She giggles.

"Mercy had a hand in it."

"Oh good. Wherever you're taking me, I envisioned myself walking around in a bra and panties, or even less," she snorts.

"And I'd be perfectly okay with that. Preferably, the naked part," I deepen my voice.

"Are we going for the entire weekend?"

"I figured just a few days wouldn't hurt. Granger is going to be in Utah with Mercy, Knox, and their parents. Nobody left at home to worry about."

Her face lights up like the sun coming out of a rainy day. "I've never been swept away for a weekend."

"No. Where did you go on your honeymoon?"

"To Logan's place. He was too busy to take me anywhere."

"His loss." I smirk, winning brownie points. I pull into the airport parking lot, finding a place in the garage.

"We're flying somewhere for the weekend?" Her eyes fill with pure childlike excitement.

"Yes." I smile, getting out and grabbing our bags.

She jumps out, sprinting around to my side. "Where are we going?"

"I've already told you it's a surprise, so quit asking. You'll have to wait until we get there."

"Man, you are cruel." She bursts out laughing, tucking her hand on the inside of my arm as I roll our suitcase through the airport doors.

I won't let her look at the tickets as we pass through security, and I forbid her to peek at the monitors for flights. "Put these in your ears." I hand her a pair of earbuds already set to listen to a playlist I downloaded for her. "These are my favorite songs," I say as she puts them in her ears.

She keeps them in for half the flight while she nods to the music and wears a gorgeous, radiant smile. She's never looked more beautiful and relaxed.

As soon as the wheels hit the runway, I call to check on Granger. They've just boarded the plane, and he's too busy playing his video games to speak to me.

"We're in Oregon?" Greer says when the pilot welcomes us to the state.

"We've got a bit of a drive to get to where we're going." I pull down our carry-on bag, and we exit the plane to the car rental area.

Once we're situated, we get on the road, and Greer yawns. "Why don't you kick back and get a nap? We have about an hour and a half drive."

"I'm going to take you up on that." She lowers her seat back and curls to her side.

The next thing you know, I'm shaking her awake. "Hey, beautiful. We've made it to our destination."

She stretches, then sits tall. "We're on the coast?" She smiles. "I've never been here before." She literally bounces in her seat like Granger does when he's all excited.

"This is Cannon Beach. My parents came here once, and they told me all about this place. I've always wanted to come here."

She leaps out and stands in front of the SUV. I reach into my bag, take out the ring, shove it into my pocket, then join her. We walk arm in arm through the quaint little town, strolling on the sandy path leading down to the ocean. The tan-colored beach area flows out a way before the harsh waves of the Pacific Ocean thunder to the shore. There's a large rock off to the left with outcroppings and caverns. Instead of the ocean floor being covered in sand, rocks and pebbles make beautiful music as the waves crash against them. Just beyond the rolling waves, sea lions have their heads sticking out of the water, barking.

"This is breathtaking." She closes her eyes and lets the evening air splash on her face as the sun sets in the distance, painting the sky orange and red.

While she has her eyes closed, I move in front of her, taking the ring out of my pocket and dropping to one knee. When she opens them, it takes her a second to see me. Her mouth gapes, and her hand flies over her mouth. "What are you doing?"

I swallow the dryness in my mouth. "Love hasn't come easy for me, and it surely isn't perfect. It isn't a fairy tale in time or pretty words written in a story-book. Love is overcoming obstacles together, of which we've already experienced. It's facing challenges together and fighting through them for something greater. It's about holding on and never letting go." I blink, unable to read her facial expression. "It's a four-letter word that's easy to spell yet difficult to define, which, by the look on your face, I'm not doing a very good job of it."

She gets on her knees with me. "Keep going," she rasps.

"It's something I've decided I don't want to live without. You've made me realize that it's worth it all. You are worth it and the only woman I want to spend the rest of my life loving." I hold out the ring.

She touches it, and her hand springs back as if she's been shocked. My gaze rocks back and forth with hers, waiting for a response. She licks her lips and smiles. "You're wrong. Every once in a while, if we're lucky, in the middle of a completely ordinary life, love gives us a fairy tale. It gave me you. I never thought I'd ever want to get married again. If I recall, I made it very clear to you in the beginning. But you've won my heart by your gentleness with me and your son, yet your fierceness turns me on." She giggles. "There is no better man for me than you, and I'd be a fool to let your love slip through my fingers."

"Will you marry me?" I hold my breath.

"Yes, River Methany, I will marry you." She flings her arms around my neck, kissing me hard and long. When she releases me, her hand shakes as she holds it out. Grasping the ring between my thumb and pointer finger, I slide it onto hers. It fits perfectly. "It's absolutely stunning," she says, staring at it.

"It was my grandmother's. She left it to my mom. When I told her I was going to ask for your hand in marriage, she shipped it overnight with a letter saying how much she loved you. She thought you'd like the connection the ring held for our family, being you desperately needed one."

"She's right. It's perfect. I've never felt more loved."

We stand, wipe the sand from our knees, and she lays her head on my shoulder as we walk hand in hand down the shoreline. As the sunsets deeper on the horizon, the air turns cooler. I feel her shiver and tuck her tight to my side.

"The house I rented is a block down from where we parked. Why don't we head back?"

"Because I never want this evening to end."

"You're cold." I turn us around. "When we get to the house, I'll keep you warm."

"Why didn't you say that in the first place?" She takes off in a sprint, laughing.

CHAPTER FIFTEEN

GREER

Two weeks have passed since River proposed to me. I've been wearing a permanent smile ever since. Things have been so good between us and eerily quiet regarding my father or Grady. The townspeople even seem happier, humming a tune as they walk along the streets.

Slipping in line at the coffee shop, I get lost in my own head while I wait. A grin curls around my lips like a lazy cat settling in a puddle of midday sunshine when I think how happy Granger was when River told him we were engaged, so much so that he cried tears of joy. He asked if he could start calling me mommy. It was so sweet. I couldn't love him any more than if he were my child. The diamond on my ring sparkles when the sun shines through the window as I hold my hand up, spreading my fingers wide to look at it, tilting my head to the side.

"I heard a rumor around town you'd gotten engaged. Seems to me that can't happen because you're still married." A familiar voice makes me flinch. Dropping my left hand in front of me, I cover it with the right, then look over my shoulder. "What do you want, Logan?"

"That's no way to greet your husband." His laugh is haughty, and he shoots me a sour look.

The grin I was wearing washes away like chalk drawings in a spring rain. I turn on my heels to face him. "Why are you here? I mean, like in the same place I am. I'm sure it's not a coincidence. And my attorney has been trying to get ahold of you to sign the damn divorce papers." My tone cracks against the air in the room, and heads spin in our direction.

"Don't make a scene," he growls lowly, taking me by the elbow, pulling me out of line.

I yank my arm from his grasp. "Take your hands off me!" I snarl.

"Calm down. All I want to do is talk to you." He plasters on a fake smile and straightens his pompous, expensive tie.

"Fine. Say what you came to say, then leave me alone." I wag my finger at him. "You can deal with me through my attorney."

"Methany is not the right man for you. Your father will never approve of him."

I squint. "You've spoken to my father recently?"

"We speak almost daily."

"What's he offered you this time to break up my happiness?" I stick my finger sharply against his chest.

He runs a hand through his dark hair. "I want you back, Greer."

"That pained you to say," I snicker.

"Look, I'm willing to not be so possessive of you and let you go back to teaching."

"Oh, really? You'll allow me to do something for myself," I scoff, planting my hands on my hips.

He grits his teeth. "You are the most infuriating woman I've ever met."

"Then tell me again why you want me back?" I drum my fingers on my chin. "I repeat. What did he offer you?"

"Lance is dead. Dustin has taken sides with your mother, and you"—he turns his nose up at me—"are worthless to him. I'm the closest thing he has left to a son. I'll inherit his fortune."

His words hum inside my head like a nest of angry hornets some fool poked with a stick. "Let me see if I can make this clear to you," I say loudly, slowly annunciating every syllable. "I want nothing to do with you ever again! I have a man who loves me for me, not what I can hand him. You're an arrogant asshole who uses people, and I won't be one of them again!"

The coffee shop bursts into a round of clapping by the patrons. "It's about time you gave him an earful," one of them says.

Logan straightens his spine and pulls his suit jacket together, buttoning it. "Mind your own business, old man," he says, with his nose in the air again.

"You have my answer. There's the door." I point.

"If you think I'm going to let that kind of money slip through my fingers because you're being stubborn, you're a fool," he spats.

"You can have every penny of his money. It's dirty, and I don't want it, but you will never, ever... I repeat, so you can get it through that thick skull of yours, never have me!"

"This isn't over!" he hollers, stomping out of the coffee shop.

"It's about time you grew some balls," Mr. Baker

says, laying his hand on my shoulder. "That man has never been anything but trouble."

"I have a feeling my suffering with him in the past is mild compared to what's coming."

"Don't let him get under your skin. I've known you for years, and in the last week I've seen you around town, it is the happiest I've ever known you to be. Marry Methany and don't look back," he says, then takes his coffee to a table by the window.

I get back in line, sending my attorney a text to expedite the paperwork. After River proposed, I called him the next day, inquiring about getting an annulment since Logan is in no hurry to put me out of my misery with him. He agreed it would be the best way to proceed, and since it was an arranged marriage and the fact he cheated, it could be done given the right Judge.

I rush out the door with my latte and fumble with my keys, unlocking the door. They fall to the ground underneath the vehicle. "Crap," I say, setting my cup on the asphalt and getting to my hands and knees. I stretch to reach them, and when I swing my arm out, I knock over my latte, and the lid flies off. "What have I done to piss you off?" I look up to the sky, then my watch. "I don't have time to wait in line again," I huff, really needing caffeine. Unlocking the

Bronco, I get inside and slam the door. As I buckle, a hand comes around me, covering my mouth. Rough edges of panic prickle my soul when I'm unable to scream.

"You wouldn't listen, so you left me no choice," Logan states with his gaze pinned on me in the rearview mirror. "I'll move my hand if you promise not to scream."

I shake my head, then bite him hard.

"Son of a..." He yanks his hand back, and his nostrils flare

"I can't believe you hijacked me in my own car!" I spin in my seat. Boiling with fury, I grind my teeth and clench my jaw so hard it hurts.

"I can't believe you freaking bit me!" He glares at me.

"What did you expect? That I'd invite you for a sleepover?" Sarcasm spills over my tongue.

He hikes a leg over the front seat, sitting on the passenger's side. "All I'm asking is for you to hear me out. Then we can both get what we want. I'd get his money, and you'd be rid of him once and for all."

"Short of killing him, I don't see how that's possible," I snarl, still ticked off.

"You know the ins and outs of all his accounts and how to finagle the books. Once he hands me an updated will, leaving me his money, you'll be done with me."

"You'll sign the divorce papers willingly?"

"Yes, but you and I have to look real, or he'll see right through it. You'll have to break up with your boyfriend. If you give River any indication it's not genuine, all bets are off." He jabs me with his finger. "I've already had my attorney throw out the annulment."

"I can't break River's heart. He'll never take me back."

"That's a chance you'll have to take. You're good in the sack. Use it in your favor."

"I hate you. You know that, right?" My face bunches together.

"We got trouble coming at two o'clock," he says with his gaze out the front window.

Chase sees me sitting in my car with Logan, and he's moseying over with a hand propped on his belt. When he gets to my side, he knocks on the window with his knuckle. I roll it down. "Is there a problem?" He sticks his head inside and glares at Logan.

"No problem at all, mister acting sheriff." He uses finger quotes.

"I wasn't talking to you," he cuts his gaze at me.

"I'm fine, really. We're just having a discussion I

didn't want the town to hear." I fake smile. "Thanks for checking on me, though."

"If you change your mind, I'll be in the coffee shop." He stands tall, but as he walks away, he stares at Logan until he's inside.

"He's going to be a problem for us," Logan exhales.

"There is no us. This game you're playing is dangerous. If my father catches you, he'll have you killed."

"That's why you'll convince him and everyone else we're back together, or I'll never release you from our marriage."

"Then I'll live in sin with River the rest of my life. It's just a crappy piece of paper, anyway. You're the one who has made me see it that way."

"Fine. If you help me, I'll also make sure your mother and brother are taken care of for the rest of their lives. As it stands right now, your mother isn't going to get anything because your dear old dad is planning on filing bankruptcy, which means he's hidden the money. Methany put a small dent in his wallet when he pulled whatever he did at the cattle auction. Alden Enterprises was unable to sell their goods this year."

"River didn't do anything. My father spread

rumors about Methany cattle, and it backfired on him."

"Not according to your old man."

"Oh, and he's so trustworthy?" I roll my eyes. "My family is better off without his dirty money."

"I didn't want to do this, but you've turned down all my other offers." He takes the keys out of the ignition. "I have all the details of your boyfriend's past. The case against him can be reopened because it never went to a trial of his peers, so him telling you he was found innocent wasn't exactly the truth. Wyatt Calhoun had a judge throw it out of court based on some verbal evidence. If you continue to refuse to help me, I'll have it resurface, and he'll have to move back to Salt Lick. He'll lose the ranch, and your father will get his land. More important-ly"—he clicks his tongue—"that son of his you admire so much will be taken away from him."

"You wouldn't dare!" I narrow my eyes. "How could you be so cruel?"

"You're forcing me." He rests back in the seat, folds his hand in front of him, and looks at his fingernails as if ruining someone's life means abso-lutely nothing to him.

"You bastard!" I yell.

"Call me what you will. Do we have a deal or

not?" He steeples his long fingers together in his lap and glares at me without blinking.

I look at him with unmitigated fury as my heart beats double-time, then I turn my head away from him with tears glossing over my vision. "You sign the divorce papers and leave River and his son alone."

"Deal," he says. "I'll expect you at my house by tonight." He opens the door. "And don't tell anyone, or all bets are off." He waves at me when he shuts the door.

What am I going to do? I can't break River's heart. He won't recover a second time. I lay my head on the steering wheel and cry. What choice do I have? I can't let him ruin River's life. He's worked so hard for everything he has, and Granger, I won't let him lose the only parent he has because of me.

Frantically wiping my eyes, I pick up the keys Logan threw on the seat before he left and start the engine. I have to pull myself together. I'm already late for school, and I have to figure out how to get through my day without falling apart.

CHAPTER SIXTEEN
RIVER

"Damn, you're dirty," Chase says as I dust off my jeans from helping drive the cattle to a new pasture.

Removing my hat, I wipe the sweat from my forehead on my sleeve. "It's ungodly hot out here today."

"Why are you driving cattle? You have men for that."

"Sometimes I enjoy it." I place my hat back on.

"Something is up with Greer." He shifts his weight in his saddle.

"What do you mean?"

"I saw her and Logan sitting in her Bronco outside the coffee shop early this morning."

"Huh, that is strange."

"I asked her if everything was alright, and she said they were just talking."

"It was probably about the divorce."

"Funny thing is, when I went into the coffee shop, people were muttering about her having a run-in with him in line. Why would she have invited him to sit in her vehicle?"

"I'll have to ask her when she gets home." I lift my wrist to look at my watch. "Which should be anytime now."

"You ride back. I'll finish up out here."

"As acting sheriff, you aren't going to be able to do this job much longer."

"Walker and Blaise are helping until the man I spoke to you about can move to Montana."

"Thanks for checking on Greer." I pull the reins to the left, turning my horse's direction to the stable. Knox is laying fresh hay for her horse when I walk my horse inside.

She stops and lays the pitchfork against the wall when she sees me. "The dust must have really been flying out there today. You're filthy."

"Nothing a shower and a change of clothes won't cure."

"I'll take care of your horse." She takes the reins and removes his saddle.

"Thanks. I need to see if Greer has made it home yet."

"She came home early and was acting kinda weird."

"How so?" I lift a brow.

"She was quiet and giving one-word answers when Mercy tried to talk to her. Granger told me she looked like she was going to cry most of the day teaching his class."

"Where is he?"

"Blaise took him into town for ice cream."

"I'll go see what's up with Greer." I stomp out, worried about her. When I open the front door, I laugh. Mercy has the music blaring, and she's acting as if she has a mic clutched in her hands, and she's dancing like nobody's business. She spins, seeing me, but doesn't stop. She simply points upstairs. I've always admired her freeness, wishing I was more like her instead of so reserved. She couldn't care less what other people think of her, and I admire it.

My boots pound on the stairs, making my way up to our bedroom. The door is cracked open, and I swear I hear sobbing. "Greer," I say her name, pushing the door open. She's sitting on the edge of the bed with her head hung down, and she's fidgeting with the ring on her finger.

"Hey," I say softly.

She sniffs, raising her head. Her eyes are puffy from crying, and she has streaks of mascara down her cheeks.

"What's wrong?" I ease myself next to her, laying my hand on top of hers. "Talk to me."

She abruptly stands. "I can't do this."

"Do what, baby?" I get to my feet and pull her chin up with my index finger curled underneath, so she'll look me in the eye.

"I can't keep your ring." She slides it off her finger, handing it to me.

"I don't understand," I stammer.

"I'm still married to Logan, and I've decided to go back to him." She walks over to the other side of the bed and drags a suitcase to the middle of the room. "I'm sorry. I never meant to hurt you. You deserve a woman who will choose you first over everything else."

My head spins with what she's saying. This can't be happening again. Squeezing my eyes shut, I pinch the bridge of my nose. "I... we..." my chest tightens as my body temperature rises, making it hard to think. I pace to the door, blocking it. "I'm baffled with why the sudden change of heart. Does this have anything to do with Logan being in your car this morning?"

"Chase told you." She pokes her tongue on the inside of her cheek and looks away.

"Answer me. Does it? You at least owe me an explanation." Anger replaces confusion in my gut.

"He told me how much he loves me and begged me to come back." Her shoulders are drooping, and she can't look me in the eye.

"You're lying. He threatened you with something, didn't he?" I close the distance between us.

Her lips tremble, and she opens her mouth, but no words come out.

"Did he threaten my life or Granger's?" I firmly grip her shoulders and bend at the knees so I can look her in the face.

She exhales through pouring tears. "Not your life, but your livelihood."

"I'll play along with whatever you need me to, but just be honest with me." I fold her into my arms, and I know she gives in when her hands wrap around my back.

"He said he'd have the case against Paige reopened if I didn't go along with him. My father promised him his estate if he'd get me away from you and have me work for him again."

I lean back to look at her. "He can't reopen the case."

"He said it never went to trial," she sobs.

"He's lying to get you to do what he wants. I had my day in court, and they found me innocent. I can't be tried again."

"Really," she sniffs. "Because he said you'd lose everything, including Granger."

I walk her back over to the bed and sit with my arm around her, and kiss her temple. "There's nothing he can do to me. I love you for doing whatever it takes to protect me and my son."

"I'd do anything for you," she wails on my chest. "I love you," she says.

"I know you do." I let her cry.

"He hijacked me in my own car!" she spews, suddenly angry.

"Logan needs you to pretend to be back together long enough to con your dad. Do I have that right?"

"He promised he'd sign the divorce papers if I helped him."

"And you believe him?" I huff.

"No." She sits, straightening her spine. "Technically, I'm still married to him, which means I have access to his precious bank accounts. Once I've found where my father has hidden his money, I'll hold Logan's accounts ransom. I can wipe them out with a click of a button."

"Damn. Remind me never to have a joint account with you." I laugh. "I'll play along and be the jilted lover, but I'm going to inform Chase so he can keep an eye on you from a distance. And, if you're ever in harm's way, all bets are off."

"What are you going to tell Granger? He's going to be so angry." Her tears flow again.

"The last thing I want is a setback with him, but I'll have to find a way to break it to him easily."

"He's going to hate me."

"There's no doubt, but when all is said and done, we'll tell him the truth. You did what you did to keep us safe. That he understands from being part of the Calhoun clan. Family first, and you are an integral part of our family."

"Thank you for loving me." She nearly knocks me over with a hug.

"It's much easier than you think." I chuckle.

"I'm going to get my divorce, and as soon as it's final, we're getting married, and I'm never letting you go." She places her hands on either side of my face and kisses me repeatedly.

I get up and put the ring in my top drawer. "I'll place this back on your finger when you're my wife."

"Logan is expecting me at his house tonight." She stands, wiping her hands over her cheeks.

"You'll be sleeping in his bed?" I growl.

"Not on your life. The pretense will only be in public and in front of my dad."

"Good, because I'd hate to have to go back to jail for a crime I actually committed. More than likely, he'll be monitoring your phone. If you need anything, call Chase. He'll know what to do and get a hold of me. Make sure you keep your gun I gave you on you at all times."

"I will. I promise," she says. "As much as I hate it, I have to go."

"Be careful, and I'll deal with the fallout here. Get the con done as fast as you can and come home to us." I kiss her, not wanting to let go.

"Thank you for not believing me when I gave you the ring back," she says, glancing over her shoulder before she hikes down the stairs.

I'm terrified for her. Her strength is amazing for someone who's had no one to believe in her until I came along. The door shuts and Mercy bolts up the steps, meeting me in the hallway.

"What did you do? Greer looked angrier than a box of frogs."

"I like how you automatically think I did something?" I snort.

"Well, did you?" Her hand flies to her hip.

It will be easier on Greer if they think I ended the relationship. She's got enough to deal with other than my family's protective hostility. "I broke off our engagement." I step sideways to get by her, moving down the stairs.

"You did what? Why?" She marches behind me.

"Her family is too much for me. It's my job to protect my son. Alden is a threat to him as long as I have a relationship with his daughter."

"I've never known you to back down from anything. Why now?" She levels a heated glare at me.

"It doesn't matter. It's over!" I push through the front door, climbing onto a four-wheeler, blasting by Mercy, who's standing on the porch yelling something at me. I hold down the lever full speed until I reach the pasture Chase is riding on. I park a distance out in order not to startle the cattle. He jerks the reins, and the horse gallops toward me.

"What's up? You drove that thing like you were being hunted." He frowns as he climbs off his horse.

"You were right to be concerned about Logan being in Greer's Bronco. Without too many questions, I need you to keep an eye on her without Logan knowing."

"The two of you are setting him up, aren't you?"

"It's a little more complicated than that. Her aim is to take her father down once and for all. Logan will fall too, and it will be a pleasure to watch. He hid in her Bronco this morning, waiting for her. If I get my hands on him, I'd likely kill him. He can't know that either of us are aware of his plan. They'll fake being back together, and she'll meet up with her father and find his money, then she'll get her divorce when she holds Logan's finances hostage."

"I'll make sure I look the other way at the crimes she's committing." He chuckles.

"I just hope she can pull it off without getting herself killed."

He props his right hand on my right shoulder. "I'll keep an eye on Logan."

CHAPTER SEVENTEEN
GREER

"So you did it. It's done. I thought you'd back out at the last minute," Logan says, gloating when I drag my suitcase inside.

I cried all the way here, so I don't have to pretend to be upset. I am. "I hope you're happy with yourself," I snark, with an exaggerated sniff.

"Poor Methany lost his woman." He loops his thumbs under his belt, bowing out his chest. "I'm the better man, anyway. You know where the bedroom is. Make yourself at home."

"I'm not sleeping in your bed. I agreed to play the part, but I won't be doing it in this home."

"You might want to rethink it because your dad is tucked away in my library."

I spin on a dime. "What? My dad has been staying in your house?"

"Our house, princess. I told you I spoke with him daily."

"I didn't think that meant you'd been hiding him out!" I yell quietly through my teeth.

He holds up his hands like a scale. "I help him. He helps me. So, I suggest you take your suitcase to our bedroom, cupcake." He slaps me on the ass, and I bawl my hands up.

"Don't touch me," I growl.

"Oh, sweetheart. I'm so glad you came back to me," he says, grabbing my hands when my father saunters into the room.

"I wouldn't believe it if I didn't see it with my own two eyes," he says, blowing out a puff of smoke from his cigar. "Perhaps Methany will be so devastated he'll go running back to Kentucky with his tail between his legs," he scoffs.

"You could have a little compassion. I broke the man's heart."

"Compassion and me ain't ever been a thing. You should know that better than anyone."

I hold back vomit when I curl into Logan's side. "It doesn't matter anymore. I'm right back where I belong with the love of my life." I plaster on a smile and bat my eyes at Logan.

"Good. Now you can get back to working on my books full-time."

"I have an obligation to the school until the end of the year, but I'll be able to work around it in the evenings and on weekends." I can't let him control every aspect of my life. An outlet and seeing Granger will be the only way I'll get through this.

"I better not hear about you even speaking to River or his family." He hits me with a harsh glare.

"His son is in my class. I can't avoid him." I shrug nonchalantly.

"Outside of the classroom, you'll have nothing to do with him, young lady." He aims his finger at me.

It took all of two seconds for his demeaning tone. "I have no need to know that Methany," as he calls him, "is doing since we are no longer together. I'm just going to take my suitcase upstairs and get settled." I point toward the marble staircase. Picking up my bag, I carry it and close the bedroom door, running to the master bathroom to hurl. "If I didn't love you so darn much, River Methany…" I cling to the side of the toilet, taking deep breaths. "It will all be over soon enough, and I'll be truly home."

Rinsing my mouth out and running my fingers through my messy hair, I walk down the stairs and hear another voice. Tiptoeing the rest of the way, I stay close to the wall and listen.

"Chase Calhoun will never see it coming. Maybe that's what they should put on his headstone." Grady belly laughs, and I hold in a gasp.

"That should be enough to send Methany back where he belongs," my father says.

"When do you plan on this going down?" Logan asks.

"Tomorrow night. My men and I will be, let's say, relieving Methany of his bulls. When they hear a rifle being shot, they'll come running. We'll be waiting for them. I'll have a man hidden in the trees. It will only take one shot to do the job." My father sounds way too pleased with himself.

"I've got to warn Chase," I whisper to myself.

"You need to hold it down some. My wife should be coming down the stairs any minute," Logan says, and I hear him walking.

Shit. "Where did you put my..." I say as if I wasn't eavesdropping, barging into the room. "Oh. I didn't realize Sheriff Grady was here too."

"You got the title right. I'll be back in charge in no time." He sticks his pudgy chin in the air.

He's disgusting.

Grady saunters over to me. "You should be happy

you came to your senses and returned to your husband. If you hadn't, you'd be tied to my bed." He runs a rough finger over my jawline.

Logan truly looks upset by the move when he bolts to my side. "That's my wife. Don't touch her," he deepens his voice to a low growl of a warning.

I'm not sure he was faking his protectiveness of me. "I am lucky I chose you," I say sweetly, batting my lashes at Logan.

"Let's not waste any more of my time. The sooner I can get out of hiding and get Grady reinstated, we'll own this town again. I had my password changed when you deserted your family for Methany." My father takes out a piece of paper from his wallet, giving it to me. "These are the new ones. It's going to take you several hours behind a computer to get everything caught up to date. There are some numbers in there I expect you to make balance just like in the old days."

"His computer is set up in my library," Logan says.

Just for show, I kiss Logan on the lips. "I'll see you in the bedroom later." I wipe his bottom lip with my finger and want to throw up again. I wink at him over my shoulder before I walk out of the living room and dash to the library. I pick up the phone on the desk, dialing Chase's number I memorized on the ride over.

"Hello," he says cautiously, not knowing this number.

"It's me. I only have a few seconds. My father is planning on shooting your bulls tomorrow night to drag you out into the open. He'll have a man in the trees aiming at you." I say all of it real fast and hang up, just in time for Logan to walk into the library.

"I see you still remembered where it was." He steps behind me, massaging my shoulders. "That was some display. I sure enjoyed your enthusiasm in making this look real."

"I told you I'd play along." My fingers tap quickly on the keyboard, gaining access to files.

"You and I may not be a real thing, but I couldn't stand watching Grady put his hands on you. You think I'm a jerk, but I saved you from him. Your father told him he could do what he wanted to you if you didn't come to see things his way. That's when I stepped in. Yes, I'm gaining financially from the deal, but I didn't want to see him harm you."

I tilt my head up to look at him. "Thank you for that," I say sincerely.

"I'll leave you at it. Dinner is being brought to the house. I'll let you know when it arrives."

As soon as he's out of the room, I gain access to my father's accounts, looking for a trail where he's hidden his money. His primary account that he deposits money from the townspeople is much lower than usual. "Good, they finally quit paying him." The fake account he had me set up funnels money in and out of a larger fund. That's the money that's been moved. It only takes me thirty minutes to locate it in an off-shore account. "Gotcha," I say, then switch over to Logan's bank account. I cross my fingers, hoping he hasn't changed the password. "Bingo!" Scanning the numbers, a large deposit was made to his account fifteen minutes ago. "That must be his reward for bringing me here." Rapidly tapping the keys, I create another account but keep it hidden from Logan's view of things. I'll simply slide into the bank when no one is looking and move the money in my name only. I lay trap number one. Now, back to the bigger fish to fry.

I spend the next hour making it look legit that I'm catching up on my father's accounts. I know he'll check behind me.

"Princess, dinner is here," Logan hollers from the hallway.

I've always hated when he calls me that, and he knows it. "Coming!" I yell, shutting the system down.

It pains me to join my father and Grady already at the table, shoveling food into their mouths. I take the seat opposing Grady so I can watch his every move, fully not expecting his socked foot to run up my thigh. Edging my hand underneath the table, I pinch him hard, and he jumps as if he's been shot.

"What the hell happened?" Logan asks, catching his drink before it topples over.

"His foot was in my crotch, and it bit him," I say, smiling.

"You better tame that girl, boy," he growls at Logan.

"You're lucky. I would've twisted your toes off. Keep your hands and feet off of my wife," he snarls. "You know I'm a possessive man," he adds in a slightly softer tone.

I reach over, holding Logan's hand. "I'd forgotten what a turn-on your possessiveness is." I almost hurl on the table.

While we eat, I listen for any clues as to other plans for harming River or his family. They keep the talk businesslike without mentioning specifics. Seems the two of them have been hiding out at Logan's since they disappeared. Smart, being the next town over. I wouldn't have guessed they'd be here.

After supper, I work on the computer for a few more hours, making adjustments I know he'll want. The smell of his cigar waifs in before he does. "I had a mind not to trust you, but I checked up on your work via my phone access. Seems you haven't lost your talent for numbers." My father's pride in my work is revolting. "I'm glad to have you back on board."

"I'm glad you're happy." My face hurts from smiling through my lie.

"With your mother and Dustin gone, that leaves you as my sole heir."

He's planning on double-crossing Logan. "As it should be," I state, continuing to type.

"I'm going to retire. I'll follow up with you tomorrow when you return from that useless job of yours." He struts out of the library with his cigar perched between his lips.

Tiptoeing to the door, I look out into the hallway to make sure Logan or Grady aren't headed this way. Calling River's number, he answers.

"Greer?"

"Yes, it's me," I say with a sigh. "Things are already falling into place. How did it go with your family?"

"It was gut-wrenching watching Granger cry."

"I'm so sorry. He's going to hate me for sure."

"He thinks it was my decision, and so does everyone else. You have enough on your plate. You don't need the wrath of my family too."

"Thank you." I swipe a tear.

"Chase told me you called him. Don't worry, we'll be ready for them. Thanks for the heads-up."

"If I hear anything else, I'll let him know. I just wanted to say good night and to tell you I love you."

"I love you too."

Shutting the computer down, I make my way to the master suite. Logan is perched against the headboard, reading a book, shirtless. "I was wondering when you were coming to bed." He lays the book on the nightstand.

I walk over, jerk the cover off the bed, and grab two pillows. "We ain't sleeping together," I say, doubling over the blanket to lie on the floor.

"Suit yourself, but the spot next to me is way more comfortable than the floor."

I should tell him my father is planning on double-crossing him, but then I'll lose the advantage over him. Once I clean out his accounts, I'll warn him, but not without a signed divorce decree in my clutches. Pulling one of River's long T-shirts I confiscated out of my bag and a pair of shorts, I walk into the bathroom to change. I'm comforted by River's scent on the shirt. After brushing my teeth, I return to my make-shift bed on the floor. "Good night," I say.

"Were things really that bad when you lived here?" Logan asks.

"Considering you were a controlling jerk and cheating on me with three other women, the answer is yes."

"The controlling part is just who I am, but I'm sorry I cheated on you. It was wrong," he says, turning out the lamp on the bedside table.

"Thank you for that," I say and roll to my side, stuffing the pillow under my head in an attempt to get comfortable. It's going to be a really long night, and I miss curling up on River's chest and falling asleep.

CHAPTER EIGHTEEN
RIVER

"I don't like anything about Greer putting herself in danger for me. She shouldn't be there," I rant to myself, pacing the porch.

Mercy comes out of the house and sits on the porch swing, rocking back and forth as she sips on pink lemonade. "I still don't understand why you broke things off with Greer. She's the best thing that ever happened to you."

I hate lying to my family. "It just wasn't going to work," I mumble.

"I'm thankful that in her heartbreak, she still reached out to Chase about the plan to kill him. Her father is pure evil."

"Chase is scouting the woods in the area where the bulls are being kept." Walker stomps the mud off his boots in the grass before he steps onto the porch. "He's going to set up in the trees with night goggles on so he'll have a bird's-eye view of the area, and we'll see Alden's men."

"Good. Blaise has five men ready to head out on four-wheelers as soon as we see them."

"What can I do to help?" Knox asks, toting a rifle.

"You and Mercy are going to stay here and guard the house. Granger needs to stay put. I don't want him outside. That includes the porch." I cut my gaze to Mercy.

"I tried calling Greer to thank her and to tell her I miss having her around, but she didn't answer the phone." Mercy's facial expression lets me know she ain't none too happy with me.

"Give her a few days. I'm sure she'll call you. It's going to be dark soon. I'll go check on Chase to see if he needs anything. Put the house on lockdown," I say, stomping to a four-wheeler.

"I have my radio if you need anything. I'll be joining Blaise," Walker hollers.

Copper comes running out of the barn and hops on the back with me. "Hold on, boy," I say, gripping the handle. The bulls are kept in a pasture on the south side of the property that's a good grazing area with lots of trees for shade to get out of the heat of the day. It's near the front of the property, which has me worried about Alden's men gaining access to the house if things don't go as they've planned, which they won't, thanks to Greer's call last night.

Chase is dressed in all black with goggles hanging around his neck, and a rifle strapped over his shoulder.

"Appears you've picked a spot," I say, parking the four-wheeler.

"I'll be able to see everything from here. I'm betting his man will set up in those trees over there." He points. "It's on Alden's property and he'll have perfect access."

"Blaise and Walker will be protecting the bulls. Mercy and Knox, the house. All the other men will be on standby outside the pasture area."

"Are you mentally ready to accept that there's a good possibility we'll kill Greer's father tonight?"

"I want that to be that last viable choice we have. I know she loves me, but that will be a hard pill for her to swallow. I'd prefer to see him rot in jail than to die at our hands."

"The girls were pretty pissed at you for ending things with Greer." He chuckles. "They'll be madder than a wet hen when they find out it wasn't real."

"Yeah, I'm sure I'll get an earful, but the fewer

people that know, the less likely she'll be caught, and I wasn't willing to risk it. I'm only sorry that it broke Granger's little heart."

"You had no other choice. He can't keep a secret." He laughs.

"At least his anger will be at me, not at Greer. That would make things even more difficult when she's his substitute teacher."

He puts his boot on the tree to climb. "I'm going to get situated. You need to get out of here, so you don't give me away."

"I'm going to wait things out with Walker and Blaise. Come on, boy." I slap my leg, getting Copper's attention after he'd hopped down to chase a squirrel.

I ride over to the wooded area where Blaise has the men scattered behind trees. Copper jumps off, running with his tail wagging toward Walker. "Hey, boy," he says, scratching him behind the ear.

"Looks like everyone is in place. It's already getting dark. Now we just wait," I tell him. Leaning against a tree, I think about Greer. What is she doing at this very moment? I can picture her biting the nail of her third finger on her left hand. She does it when she's worried about something. The poor nail is nothing more than a nub. I have to keep telling myself this will all be over soon, and she'll be home where she belongs.

It's funny how quickly I've gotten used to her being around and learned all her little nuances, such as how she prefers her coffee in a larger mug full of flavored cream. The way she squeezes the toothpaste from the top drives me insane. I leave the shower door open after I've gotten out of it. She doesn't like that, and I've heard her in the bathroom ranting to herself about it as she closes it. The best thing is how she entangles her feet with mine and lays her head on my chest to fall asleep. I'm hotter than Hades, but I don't dare move an inch because I love the feel of her body next to mine. It'd be better if she didn't radiate heat, but I'll live with it.

"Whatever you're thinking about has put a smile on your face." Walker chuckles. "I know you've called it quits with Greer, but she sure looked good on you. You wouldn't mind if I asked her out, would you?" He raises both of his brows.

"I would absolutely hate it," I say, pushing off the tree.

"I thought so." He chuckles. "You may have Mercy and Knox convinced you two are over, but I don't believe you for one hot minute." He taps his finger to his temple.

"Did you see that?" I ask, moving out from under the tree. "I saw a vehicle coming down the road, and then it turned its lights off."

My radio crackles. "They're here," Chase says. "There are three trucks with their lights turned off, following one another in this direction."

"Copy that," I respond on the radio.

Walker and Blaise radio the men to be ready. I get on with Mercy, letting her know things are fixing to go down. Once the trucks are parked, eight men get out and line up along the fence line with flashlights. Alden steps out of the middle vehicle and waves his arms around, giving orders.

Copper takes off in a full run, barking. "Damn it," I say. I start for the four-wheeler to chase after him, but Walker stops me. "If you show your face, they'll know someone tipped us off. It will put Greer in danger."

I back off, waiting to hear the first shot, fully expecting to lose one of our bulls, but when a rifle is fired, Copper cries out. "I'm going to kill the bastard," I snarl, climbing on the four-wheeler. Racing toward them, the other men come out of the woods with their rifles aimed. I can hear another shot in the direction where Chase is hiding. My headlights are aimed at Alden's face. He covers his eyes with his hands and darts toward his vehicle. We exchange gunfire with his men. A few drop to the ground and others escape to their trucks. Alden speeds away, and our men surround the other vehicles, keeping them from leaving. I comb the area for Copper but don't see him.

"Copper!" I yell at the top of my lungs, stopping the four-wheeler.

"I see something moving in the high grass," Walker says, out of breath from running the distance of the pasture.

I pull the lever, bolting me forward. My heart thuds hard when I see Copper lying in the grass covered in blood. Jumping off, I run over to him, and he cries, lifting his head.

"It's okay, boy," I say softly. Gently picking him up, I carry him, place him on my lap, and drive to the barn. Laying him in a soft pile of hay, I snatch my phone from my pocket and call our veterinarian, who says he'll be here within twenty minutes.

Pulling cabinets open, I take out a towel and grab a bucket full of water. I sit, putting Copper's head in my lap. Wiping him gently, I can see the damage. He has a bullet hole in his left hip. He yelps when I apply a little pressure.

"I know it hurts. I'm sorry. You're going to be

alright, I promise," I say against his ear. He pants in pain and tries to lick his wound. "I've got you. It's alright." I don't know whether I'm trying to convince him or myself.

Twenty minutes seemed like an eternity until the vet arrived. "Let me look at him," he says, squatting with his medical bag beside him.

I hold Copper tight so he won't move.

"The bullet is still inside him. I need to remove it. From the looks of it, he'll be okay once I get it out and get some fluids in him, but I won't know for sure until I see some X-rays. I can't remove the bullet here. He'll have to come with me."

Cradling him in my arms, I pick him up and carry him to the vet's truck, laying him on the seat. I nuzzle his snout with my face. "You'll be okay," I whisper. "I'd go with you, but I need to take care of things here first."

"I have your number. I'll call you when I know more."

"Thanks, Doc," I say, shutting the door and storming to the four-wheeler. Laying on the speed, I fly to where I left the men. Swirling blue lights and an ambulance have arrived. Chase has several men in handcuffs, and his men are putting them in the backseat of squad cars.

"Did we get Alden?" I ask, parking next to him.

"No, but we have several of his men. We killed one man. Three others were injured. Not including the sniper that was supposed to shoot me. I could see him in my scope. I took a shot and hit him in the shoulder. We could use him to testify against Alden."

"If he thinks Greer tipped him off, she's in danger." I kick the dirt.

"He has no reason to suspect her. He took the first shot, and we came running, just like he planned. Did you find Copper?"

"Yeah." I exhale. "He's with the vet. He took a shot to the hip. The vet thinks he'll be alright."

"He's a good dog." He slaps me on the shoulder.

"I'll get out of your way and let you take care of things. I'm going to go check on the girls and Granger."

"WE HEARD GUNFIRE. IS EVERYONE ALRIGHT?" Knox asks, meeting me at the front door.

"Yeah. The only injury sustained on our part was Copper. He charged them, trying to protect us."

"Oh no!" Mercy cries.

"He's going to be okay. I called the vet, and he

came out and got him. The bullet hit him in the hip."

Knox hauls the rifle from behind the door to her shoulder. "Who did it? I'm going to kill them myself."

"Hold on, Calamity Jane. Alden got away."

"That bastard! Shooting an innocent dog!" Mercy is all fire mad.

"Copper got shot?" Granger wails from the steps in his pajamas.

I hold my arms out, and he comes running. "He's going to be alright, I promise. The vet is taking good care of him." He's been so mad at me since I told him about Greer. I'm happy he's letting me comfort him. "You ladies need to get some rest. Chase is handling things." I walk Granger up the stairs and place him in his bed.

"Can we go see Copper?" he sniffs.

I drag my phone out and hit video call to the vet. He's used to late-night cattle calls from me and uses video all the time.

"How is he?" I ask.

"The bullet has been removed. He's fortunate it only hit muscle and nicked an artery. I've hung fluids, and he's just waking up. The dog can come home tomorrow on antibiotics. He'll be sore, but no permanent damage." He turns the camera on Copper.

"See, I told you he'd be good."

He wipes his nose with his hand. "I love him," he says.

"I know you do. Thanks for taking care of him," I tell the vet and hung up. "Why don't you try to get some sleep?" I kiss his forehead.

"Can I sleep with you? I'm afraid I'm going to have bad dreams." His mouth turns down into a frown.

I pull back the covers. "Come on," I say, and he runs to my room.

CHAPTER NINETEEN

GREER

I've paced the library floor all night wanting to call River to find out what happened. My fingernail is almost completely gone from me gnawing on it. I wanted to follow my father when he left, but I couldn't shake Grady and Logan, so I've hidden out among the books in this room.

The clock strikes midnight with a loud chime, then the door slams, hearing my father bellow for Grady. Softly padding down the hallway, I follow the sound of another banging door from Logan's office. Making sure the coast is clear, I press my ear to the door.

"What happened?" Grady asks.

"Methany's damn dog came charging at me. He took a hunk of meat out of my leg. Shortly after that, his men showed up with rifles. I got the hell out of there."

"We're any of your men killed?"

"I don't know, nor do I rightly care," he huffs.

"Did this go down on your property or Methany's?"

"The dog attacked me on Methany's land, but the men were on my property. What difference does it make? My damn leg hurts!" he hollers.

"Your men weren't trespassing, so they had no right to bear arms against them. I'll file a complaint with Chase. He'll have no choice but to arrest his own men."

"I knew I kept you in my wallet for a reason," my father tells him.

"If they all showed up at once armed, do you think someone tipped them off?"

"Oh shit!" I mouth.

"Who else knew besides the two of us?"

"Logan," Grady says.

"Why would he rat us out to Methany? I've paid him a large sum of money to keep his mouth shut. He ain't gonna risk what he believes he's getting. There is no way in hell I'm putting that idiot in my will."

I knew it. He's been lying to Logan to manipulate him into getting what he wants.

"What about that daughter of yours? Could she have overheard us talking?" Grady says. Then I hear footsteps. I quickly dart into an empty room, hiding behind the door.

The office door opens, and Grady's shoes tread on the wood floor, heading in my direction. The light pops on, and I hold my breath, standing stock-still until it goes back off and his footsteps lead back to the office.

Clutching my stomach, I exhale tons of fear. If he thinks I tipped them off, I'm a goner. My entire body trembles as I sneak into the hallway and tiptoe up the stairs to the bedroom, quietly closing the door behind me. I nearly jump out of my skin when I hear the click of the lamp followed by the light coming on.

"Why are you sneaking around the house this time of night?" Logan narrows his stare at me.

"You can't trust my father. I know he's paid you a lot of money, but he plans on double-crossing you. I just overheard him tell Grady that he has no intention of putting you in his will."

"You're lying," he snarls. "Why should I believe a

word you say?" He tosses the cover back and sits on the edge of the bed.

"When we were together, did I ever lie to you?"

He moves his mouth from side to side. "Not that I know of."

"I'm not lying now, either." I sit beside him.

"Damn it!"

"I overheard their plan to kill Chase, and I warned him. They were ambushed by River's men, and now Grady has told my father he suspects you or I told them."

He falls back on the bed, pulling his hair. "They'll kill us both."

I get up, lock the door, and push the dresser in front of it. "I have a gun in my purse. If they get in here, I'll use it."

"You'd kill your own father?" He sits.

"I only have to stop him, not kill him. We need to combine our brains and come up with a plan."

"If you think I'm signing the divorce papers now, you're crazy."

I take out my cell phone. "On my lunch break at school today, I stopped by the bank. Funny thing, I'm still on all your bank accounts because legally, we're still married."

His eyes bulge. "What did you do?"

Opening the link to his account, I hold my phone in front of him. "You weren't even smart enough to change the password." His accounts show a hundred dollars each.

"What did you do with my money?" he seethes with his face turning the color of a plum.

"It's safe and sound, and I'll return it when I have the signed papers in my hand and a copy mailed to my attorney."

"You are your father's daughter," he snarls. And I slap him across the face.

"I'm nothing like my father! I'm tired of being used and abused by men like you! I stand up for myself and somehow in your mind that makes me the bad guy! I've had enough!"

His shoulders sag, and his head droops. "You're right. I've been a greedy-ass man who never cared about your feelings."

I'm stunned by his admission. "You have the chance to change that now. Help me stop my father and Grady."

He stands without a word, walks over to his wall safe, and spins the wheel until it opens. Taking out a file, he lays it on his dresser and takes a pen from a drawer, signing papers. "Here are the divorce papers. You win. I'm the loser here because you really are a good woman." Holding the file out, I take it from him.

"Thank you," I say.

"I'll help you, and then I'll be out of your life for good." He walks back over to the bed. "You should sleep with the gun under your pillow," he says before lying down, drawing the covers over him.

I pick up my makeshift cot and throw the pillows on the bed next to him, lying on top of the comforter. Reaching over, I hold his hand. "Thank you." A few minutes later, he's snoring. I toss and turn for the next hour, concerned about River and his family.

Easing out of bed so as not to wake Logan, I pad to the bathroom, close the door, and hit River's name on my phone.

"Hey," he whispers.

"I've been worried sick."

"We're all okay," he says, and I hear a door close. "Granger is sleeping in my bed."

"Daddy came back here in a rage, yelling and carrying on at Grady."

"Wait. They're at Logan's place with you?"

"He's been hiding him since he went missing."

"Get out of that house right now. If he thinks you

tipped us off, there's no telling what he'll do." His voice rises with fear.

"I'm barricaded in Logan's room. Daddy plans on denying all the promises he made to Logan, and I told him about it. He's on my side now."

"I don't like this one bit," he bites out.

"He signed the divorce papers right in front of me."

"A lot of good that does if you ain't alive to marry me," he snaps.

"I'll live to marry you, River Methany." My words are sweet to calm him down.

"You have until tomorrow evening to act on whatever plan it is your scheming. After that, I'm coming in after you with a loaded gun."

"I've already located his offshore dealings. I've set up another account that it will dump into tomorrow at the close of business. He'll never know the money's gone until Monday. He'll be so pissed. There will be a donation made in his name to support the wealth and healthcare of abused women and children."

He bursts out laughing. "That's outstanding!"

"We will dedicate it to Paige," I add softly.

He inhales sharply. "Thank you."

"I figured his dirty money needed to go to a good cause."

"You and your mother will be left with nothing."

"I'm good with that, and my mother will be just fine without it."

"I wish you were here so I could kiss you."

"I wish I was there so you could screw my brains out." I giggle. "Adrenaline rushes really make you horny."

"That too." He chuckles. "I love you, Greer. Don't go getting yourself killed before we legally change your last name to mine."

"Greer Methany. I love the sound of that." I sigh.

I hear Granger scream. "I gotta go."

"Love you," I say before he hangs up.

I tiptoe back to bed and sleep the rest of the night after talking to him. When I wake up the next morning, the dresser has been moved, and Logan is gone. Rushing to dress, I slap my bare feet on the marble tile on the way to the kitchen.

Daddy is sitting at one end of the large kitchen bar reading a newspaper, and Grady is at the other end, sipping on coffee.

"Good morning." I try to sound chipper. "Where's my darling husband?"

"He had to go to the office for a few hours,"

Daddy says, without taking his eyes off the newspaper.

I pour a cup of coffee with my back to them.

"There was an incident at the Methany ranch last night," he says.

"Oh, really?" I say, turning to face them. "Not that it's my problem anymore, but what happened?"

"His men shot up my associates."

"We're they on his property?"

"No," Grady says. "I'll be having charges drawn against them."

"You wouldn't happen to know more than what you're saying? His men knew our plan."

"How would I know? I wasn't informed of what you were doing." I lift a shoulder in denial.

"Hmmm..." is all my father grunts.

"I've got class in an hour. I'll see you gentlemen later," I say, sashaying to the front door and grabbing my sandals. I watch in my rearview mirror as I drive off, making sure I'm not followed. When I park in the employee parking lot, I check my phone to double-check on transferring monies to see that it goes through as planned.

Walking around the side of the building, I bump into a man. "Excuse me," I say. I know everyone in this town, and I've never seen him before. He appears to be lost. "Are you new here?" I ask.

"You could say that. My son is enrolled at this school, and I thought I'd check it out."

"You have to register at the front office to be wandering around on the property."

"I've already done that." He flashes a name tag they issued him

Something about him seems off, so I make a mental note. He's about five feet eleven, a tad bit shorter than River. A scar runs the length of his chin. He has dark brown hair, but I can't tell the color of his eyes because his sunglasses obscure them. "Parents aren't allowed back here. How about I escort you to the front of the building where the kids are being dropped off? You can see the process, so you'll be familiar with it."

"Thank you, kindly, ma'am," he says with an upturn of the corner of one side of his mouth.

I take him to the front and rush to the office to see which class they have assigned me to today. I'm relieved when it's not Granger's. He'll have a million questions, and I have too much on my mind to answer him.

Thankfully, the day flies by, and before I know it, the last bell rings. I purposely avoid the pickup line, so I don't have to see Granger or one of River's family members. Hurrying home, I get a bad feeling the minute I walk in the door.

Logan greets me with a hug. "Hey, baby," he shouts, then whispers in my ear. "Grady is pissed because Chase refused to file charges, and he has a warrant out for your father's arrest. His own men turned him in for planning to kill the sheriff."

I feel for my gun in my purse. "It's now or never." I check my watch. It's five p.m. on the dot, which means they have moved the money.

Laying my hand on the inside of his elbow, we walk into the library, where my father is clicking away on the computer. "It's about damn time you got home!" He slams it shut.

Taking a deep breath, garnering all of my courage, I tell him, "You're done in this town." I fold my arms over my chest, and Logan tucks his hands in his pocket.

"What the hell are you babbling about?" He rises, with steam already exploding from his ears.

"Your hold on these people and me is over. Grady is never being reinstated, and you're penniless and can no longer bribe anyone."

"Get your wife under control," he snarls at Logan, spearing him with squinted eyes.

"She's no longer my wife. I signed the divorce papers, freeing her from both of us." There is no fear in his tone.

"I paid you a ton of money to keep her. You can forget inheriting my fortune," my father snaps, pounding his fist on the desk.

Logan laughs. "You had no intention of leaving me anything."

"Did you not hear what I said?" I walk over to him, taking his focus off of Logan. "You have no money."

He glares at me, then at Logan, and it finally registers. The laptop flies open, and he logs into his account. "What have you done?" he howls with spit coming out of his mouth.

"You're so generous to have donated every last penny to abused women and children, being that you're so good at both."

He yanks open a drawer, pulling out a gun, but I've already taken mine out and aiming it at him.

"You wouldn't shoot your own father," he sneers.

"I could say the same about your daughter." I don't waver. "Call the sheriff," I order Logan.

"He was called prior to you getting home," he says, smirking.

"Appears we have a standoff," Grady utters behind us.

I don't take my aim off my father. I know if I do, he'll kill me. "Get him out of here," I tell Logan.

Grady dodges Logan's grasp and runs down the hallway. A loud crash echoes through the house as they scuffle. "You and I can come to some sort of agreement," my father says, laying on the charm. "We're family, after all."

"That time has long passed. The only thing I want is for you to be behind bars, paying for your crimes."

He lays his gun on the desk. "It was you that warned Methany."

"I love him, and I'm never going to let you hurt him," I snap, keeping my finger on the trigger.

"You ain't the kind of woman a man loves long, so enjoy it while it lasts," he snorts.

"There you go, assuming you know better than anyone else. You do not have an inkling of what kind of woman I am or what I'm capable of. You've sorely misjudged me."

He acts as if he's going to turn around, and he dives for the gun. I adjust my aim, firing once, hitting him in the knee. He crumples to the ground, wailing in pain. "You bitch!" he screams. "You shot me!"

I pick up his gun with a tissue and put it back in the drawer, and stand over him. "You're lucky it was just your knee," I spat.

The front door bashes against the wall as it's busted open. "She's in the third room down the hall," I hear Logan telling someone.

Chase enters the room wearing a bulletproof vest with his gun gripped in his hands. "You alright?" he asks when he sees my father withering in pain.

I open the desk drawer. "I'm sure this is the stolen gun that Grady said disappeared."

"She shot me! I want her arrested!" my father yells.

"It was self-defense." I smack my lips.

Chase radios for an ambulance. I step out of the room to check on Logan. He's got a lump on the side of his head and an eye that's already turning black. Grady is out cold on the tile floor.

"Thank you." I wrap my arms around his waist.

"I want you to know that Methany is a lucky man," he says, tucking a lock of hair behind my ear.

A police officer takes over for Chase, and he confronts Logan. "You're under arrest, too, for forcing your way into her vehicle and aiding a criminal."

"I'm not pressing charges. He helped me today." I stand in front of him, facing Chase.

"I'll make note of his assistance, but he still had a criminal living in his home."

"It's alright, Greer." He touches my arm. "I deserve it for ever trusting your father."

A gurney comes in, and then my father is being carried out, along with Grady. "They'll get the care they need, then they'll be taken to jail," Chase says.

"Do you need me down at the station? I'd really love to go home." I fold my hands together, pleading.

"You can come to the station tomorrow. I think you've better things to do." He smiles, and I hug him. "Thank you. Do me a favor and don't call River. I want to be the one to tell him it's all over."

"After everything you've done, it's the least I can do. My lips are sealed, but the local press will be all over this, so make it quick."

"I will." I step to leave, but he grabs my hand.

"What you did was brave. Never do it again," he says firmly.

"Let's hope I never have to."

CHAPTER TWENTY

RIVER

"Copper's home!" Granger flies down the stairs, greeting me in the living room as I ease the dog down into his bed.

"Easy," I tell Granger as he hugs him tight. "You're going to have to be extra gentle with him for a few days."

Copper's tongue laps all over his face, and Granger is eating it up. "I'm so glad he's home."

"Me too." I rub the dog's head.

Mercy pops her head into the room. "There's a Bronco out front," she says. "Do you want me to run interference?" Her gaze lands on Granger for a split second, then on mine.

I stand. "Why don't you help Aunt Mercy fix Copper something to eat?"

"I'm not ready to leave his side yet," he whines, looking up at me.

"He won't get better if he doesn't eat," Mercy says, holding her hand out for him. He takes it, and they walk out of the room as there's a knock on the door.

Opening it, Greer looks worn out yet somehow radiant. "It's over." She exhales as if she's been holding in words on the drive over, then flings her arms around my neck. "My father and Grady have both been arrested."

"Thank God," I say, breathing a warm breath on her neck and holding on to her at the waist. "Are you okay?"

She steps back and smiles. "I'm penniless and never felt more free."

Taking her by the hand, I step out onto the porch, closing the door, not wanting Granger to hear the dirty details. "What happened?"

"He was infuriated about me giving his money away and pulled a gun on me, but I was ready for him. He tried to sweet talk me and then dove for his gun. I couldn't make myself kill my own father no matter what he'd done, so I aimed my gun downward, shooting him in the knee."

I run my hands down her body, spinning her around. "Did he hurt you?"

"Physically, I'm fine. Logan's busted up from fighting with Grady, but he'll be alright. Chase took him into custody for aiding my father."

"I'm surprised Chase didn't call me."

"I asked him not to. I wanted to tell you myself so you'd see I'm okay. My father won't be able to hurt you or anyone else anymore."

Placing my hands on either side of her face, I kiss her, and she returns it with every ounce of love I feel for her. "Thank you. I can't imagine going against my family like you did. You're an incredible woman, and I'm so thankful to have you in my life."

"Ditto," she says.

"I thought you two broke up," Granger says through the screen in the window.

"Come here," I say, opening the door for him to join us on the porch. "Sit." I point to the porch swing. He sits in the middle with me on one side of him and Greer on the other. "I made up a story to protect you and Greer."

"You lied," he says, crossing his arms. "I get in trouble when I lie."

"Lying is a bad thing, yes. Sometimes it's necessary to protect the ones you love."

Greer takes his hand in hers. "I'm sorry we lied to you, but your daddy is right. We did it to keep all of us safe. The danger is over now, so we can be a family."

"You're still going to marry my daddy?" He peers up at her.

"Yes, but not only your daddy." She gets on her knees in front of him. "I know you don't have my eyes or my smile, but I knew the day I met you how much I loved you. That will never change. You're not my blood, but I want you to be my boy... my son. You and your daddy make me a better woman, and I don't want to ever be away from either of you again." She bites her bottom lip, waiting for his response.

"I want to marry you too," he shouts, and we all enjoy a good laugh.

I disappear to my room to fetch her ring. When I come back downstairs, Granger is curled up next to her on the swing, chatting with her as if she's been gone a year. I hand the box to him. "Do you want to put it on her finger this time?"

His face lights up with a genuine smile. "Yes," he says, taking it from me. Greer holds out her hand, and he slips it on her finger. "This means you can never take it off or leave us."

"I promise to love both of you for the rest of my days." She hugs him hard as tears slip down her cheek.

"How about you let me hug my future wife." I laugh, peeling him off of her. "Go check on Copper," I tell him, and he skips off one happy little boy.

"That kid is the best," Greer sniffs on my shoulder.

"He is a good kid, and I feel the same way you do. He ain't my blood either, but he's mine by choice. Definitely my boy. I do see myself through his eyes, more and more every day. He's much bigger than any plans I ever had in my life. I'm a much better man because of him."

"We're all pretty darn lucky," she says right before kissing me.

I slide my hands to her ass, pulling her into me. "We keep this up, we're going to be naked right here on the porch," I rasp on her lips.

"Granger told me the good news." Mercy bursts onto the porch. "Of course I'm mad as hell at you for keeping me out of the loop," she adds.

Greer lays her lead on my chest, and I don't let go because she's the only thing hiding the bulge in my Levi's. "It was necessary," I moan.

She grins. "I'm just glad none of it was real." She goes to hug Greer, but I don't let her. "You gotta wee problem there, cowboy?" She giggles, staring at where our bodies are glued together.

"How about you go back inside and give us a minute?" I huff. "To you, it's a big problem," I groan.

"I'd like at least an hour," Greer snorts.

"You fit right in," Mercy howls, then goes inside.

"An hour, huh?" I nuzzle my nose against the side of her neck.

"I said at least, cowboy." She slides her hand between us, cupping my cock.

"We can slip inside while Mercy has Granger preoccupied," I growl.

"I was thinking we could break in my Bronco." She smiles, tugging my hand.

"Whatever you say, baby."

GREER IS STRAIGHTENING her dress and covering her hand on her throat to cover where my whiskers rubbed against her fragile skin, leaving red marks as she climbs out of the back of the Bronco.

"I'll grab your bags," I say, grinning.

"You think it's funny, don't you?" She slaps my ass.

"I love the fact that you're pink because of me." I puff my chest out with pride. "It says you're mine and don't forget it."

"Another possessive cowboy, except this time, I love it." She places a quick kiss on my cheek.

Knox rides up on her horse. "I heard the good news," she says.

"Good news travels fast around here," I comment.

"You two may want to purchase curtains for that Bronco. Seeing your white ass is blinding." She laughs, shielding her eyes.

Greer roars. "We should be a tad more discreet."

"Trust me, with our family, it ain't nothing we all haven't seen before. My mom and dad used to get an earful from his parents. They created a makeshift hot tub down by the river behind River's house. They'd sneak off every chance they got. I can't tell you how many times we caught them."

"That's a great story. It's good to hear how much your parents love one another. I'm kinda jealous." Greer tucks her hand into mine.

"Don't be. Seeing your daddy's tush ain't a fond memory," she snickers.

"Now that you two ladies have thoroughly enjoyed walking down memory lane at my expense, what do you say we all go out and celebrate?"

"That's a great idea," Knox states, pulling on the reins and riding back to the stable.

"I love your family." Greer lays her head on my shoulder.

"Most days I do, others not so much." I chuckle.

She goes upstairs to unpack her clothes while I gather up the troops, informing them that the threat to the ranch and our family is over. No more being stuck on the property, and we can lighten up on the security. Walker informs the ranch hands, giving them some time off.

Chase pulls into the drive, stomping in my direction by the corral. "You heard the news?"

"Yeah. It's great to know Alden and Grady are finally behind bars."

"Not that news," he scowls, removing his sunglasses.

"Your father's been trying to call you for the last hour."

"Crap," I say, feeling my pocket. "My phone must be in the Bronco."

"Darrell got paroled," he states.

"Just when I thought things were going to settle down." I blow out a long breath. "When did this happen?"

"Five days ago. His attorney failed to notify yours."

"He doesn't know where we're living. I'm not

going to let the news interfere with my good mood. We're all going out to celebrate that it's finally over. This land is ours without any more hassles."

"Greer did a good thing, but she's lucky she wasn't killed in the process." He props his hand on my shoulder.

"Just tell me that there's no possible way he's getting off."

"His attorney will fight it, of course, but with what Greer has on him, he won't be free for a really long time. We will prosecute Grady right along with him."

"What about Logan?"

"Greer didn't press charges. He'll still be held accountable for hiding Alden, but he has no priors. I'm sure he'll only get a slap on the hand. He ended up helping Greer in the end."

"And he signed the divorce papers." I clap him on the back as I mosey to the house. "Let's not mention Darrell just yet. I'd like everyone to enjoy their evening without being afraid."

"Whatever you say." He falls in line behind me. I run up the stairs to the bedroom to check on Greer. She has her head tipped over, brushing her hair. She flings it up, and she has a fresh layer of lip gloss on.

"Hey," she says, looking at me in the mirror behind her.

"You look beautiful." I slide my arms around her waist, resting my chin on her shoulder. "Especially with me next to you."

"It's the only place I want to be." She smiles.

"What do you say after our celebration with the family, we talk about setting a wedding date? I'm not one for long engagements."

"Are we talking months or weeks?" She lifts a brow.

"I was thinking days." I kiss her collarbone. "Why wait one minute longer than we have to? I vote on getting married here on the ranch."

She turns in my arms. "I'd marry you anywhere."

"I like the sound of that." Our lips meet.

"We've already been caught once today." She giggles. "We shouldn't keep them waiting, or Granger's going to come hunt us down."

As if on cue, Granger bounces through the door. "I'm ready!" he squeals, fidgeting with the button on his collar.

"You look mighty handsome," I tell him, squatting. "You didn't have to get all dressed up."

"I wanted to. It's a special occasion. It ain't every

day a boy gets a momma." His lips land on my cheek.

"You're gonna make me cry," I sniff.

"None of that." I pick him up, and Greer snuggles under my arm.

"Do I get to have a beer to celebrate?" He bats his eyes.

"A root beer." I chuckle.

"I'll have one with you. I don't like the taste of beer anyway." Greer tweaks his nose.

"We'll all have root beers. How's that?"

"Speak for yourself. After the week I've had, I'm shooting down two beers at minimum," Chase says, coming into the bedroom with Mercy behind him.

I set Granger on his feet, and Mercy escorts him out. Chase looks at Greer, then me, clearing his throat. "Would you excuse us?" he says to her.

"Sure. I'll just go downstairs and wait for the two of you."

He waits until she closes the door. "Did you tell her about Darrell?"

"No. We've already discussed this. I don't want to worry her about another thing."

"I know I'm being overly cautious, but hear me out."

I puff out my cheeks. "I'm listening."

"If by chance, Darrell finds out your location, the first thing he's going to do is come after Granger. Her being at the school, I think she should be informed."

"I'll tell her, but not until there's a need to. I'd like to at least enjoy the weekend without having to be fretting about something else."

He flexes his jaw. "Alright. It's your call, but if I receive word that he's MIA, I'll tell her myself."

"I appreciate your concern. You've had a rough start as acting sheriff, with shooting Lance and the arrests of Alden and Grady. Let's go out and forget about the job, just for tonight. I'm proud of you, man." I place a firm grip on his shoulder.

"Thanks," he says. "You're right. We deserve a night off. All of us."

CHAPTER TWENTY ONE

GREER

I've got the Monday morning blues, not wanting to be at work today. At least I got assigned to Granger's class. It's been a joy watching him light up, telling all his friends that I'm marrying him and his daddy. And this weekend... well, I have no words other than it was perfect. We all had so much fun celebrating at the restaurant together. Chase even forfeited his beer when Granger handed him a root beer. They all cave to the little man. He's got every single one of them wrapped around his finger, myself included. I hope one day he'll realize how lucky of a young man he is to have so many people that love him.

I know it's not possible, but I swear, sometimes when I look at his eyes, I see River. Maybe it's only because he's learned to mimic River's expressions, but there's a hint of him in the twinkle of his eyes. I've never really given much thought to having a child of my own, but part of me aches to give one to River. He's such a good father, and I'd love to see him raise a little girl. He'd damn near kill any boy that would even look at his daughter. I can see him taking her to a father and daughter dance and growling at the boys smiling at her.

"Ms. Alden, I have to pee." The boy sitting next to Granger is bouncing in his seat.

Opening the drawer of the desk, I take out the hall pass. "Go ahead," I tell him.

Granger follows him to my desk. "You must've been thinking about my daddy. Timmy has been hollering for five minutes that he has to pee."

I giggle. "You're right, I was, but don't tell anybody. I promise not to daydream anymore."

The bell rings. "Recess!" Granger yells, pumping his hands in the air.

I stand. "Alright, everybody line up. We can't go until Timmy returns."

The children line up in a single file, and the volume goes up. It's good to hear them laughing and playing with one another. Timmy comes back, and we walk down the hallway out the back door to the playground. They scatter like ants hunting for food. I sit with one of the other teachers on a bench, watching the children. Out of the corner of my eye, I see a man sitting in a vehicle, wearing dark sunglasses. It's the same father I met the other day checking out the school. I can't tell for sure, but it appears he's looking at the playground.

"Do you recognize that man as the parent of one of your kids?" I ask the other teacher, tilting my head in the man's direction.

"No. I've never seen him before."

Rising slowly, I nonchalantly walk over to the fence while keeping my attention on the children. He suddenly rolls up his window and shoves his car into gear, moving down the road.

"That's odd," I say to myself. I move back to the bench. "Are you certain you don't recognize him?"

She shakes her head.

I stand watch over the children until the bell rings. They go inside and get in line at the water fountain. Snatching my phone from my desk, I call the principal's office, asking if they'd issued any school passes to a parent and let her know what I saw. She assures me she will have security check it out.

We get settled back into class, and I receive a text

from Mercy, asking if I'd mind bringing Granger home from school today. I respond with no problem. The children are working on art for our room. The assignment was for them to draw something that makes them happy. I see pictures of ice cream, horses, swimming, a kid playing football with his father, and a child on a bike. When I get to Granger's desk, I look over his shoulder.

"Who is that?" I ask, pointing to a small child in a woman's arms. "That's my baby sister." He smiles up at me with a mischievous gleam in his eyes.

"You don't have a baby sister." I laugh.

"Nope. But one day I will, and she'll make me happy." His grin is so wide it's covering his entire face, bleeding up to his ears.

"Carry on," I say, smiling along with him.

The last bell of the day rings, and children hop up, getting their backpacks on. Granger does the same. "I'll be taking you home today, so you'll have to hang out with me for an hour or so if that's alright with you."

"Sure," he answers, lifting one shoulder.

"I'm not on pickup duty. If you want to draw on the blackboard, you can." I know how much he loves it. "If you'll let me get my work done, I'll take you for ice cream."

"Yes!" He fist bumps the air.

The kids all leave, and Granger takes the colored chalk from my drawer as I stack the papers from today and review tomorrow's classwork. By the time I'm done, he's drawn a picture of the ranch on the blackboard. There's a stick figure standing in the middle of a corral with a horse. "Is that your uncle Walker?" I ask, resting my hand on his shoulder.

"He finally broke that stubborn horse," he says.

I ruffle his hair. "You ready for ice cream?"

He smiles, tucking the chalk back into my desk. "We better not tell my daddy. He'll say it will spoil my supper."

"I won't say a word." I zip my lips, and he takes my hand as I toss my purse on my arm. He leads me down the hallway and out the back door of the building that locks automatically behind me.

"I love your Bronco," he states, climbing inside and buckling his seat belt.

"Better than your daddy's new truck?" I ask, starting the engine and backing out.

"Yes, but we don't have to tell him that either." He smirks.

"Do you keep a lot of secrets from your father?" I cut my gaze at him.

"Only the things that will get me in trouble." He

laughs. He reaches over and turns up the radio. His little head bebops to an upbeat country song.

When we make it down Main Street, I parallel park out in front of the red brick building that takes up the entire block. It used to be a department store with squeaky old wooden floors. It closed a few years ago, and an investor bought it and remodeled it into individual shops. There are eight narrow shops, including the ice cream parlor, and a restaurant on the end. To keep the authenticity of the building, there are no windows other than where the storefront used to be. Each shop only has a glass front door and an access door on the back. If you were a stranger to town, you'd never know it was an ice cream shop other than the painting on the door. The owner, Etta Mae, who I've known since I was Granger's age, rents the space. She painted a colorful ice cream cone on the door, and on the top is the name of the place. It reads in fancy lettering, The Sweet Spot. I grab my wallet and phone out of my purse and jump out.

The bell jingles when Granger rushes in the door, getting in line behind one of the kids from his school.

"Hi, sweetie," Etta Mae says, waving me behind the counter. I walk around, and Granger follows me.

"How are you?" I ask, hugging her neck. She recently lost her oldest son, who was forty, to cancer, and she had a friend serving up ice cream.

"I'm alright as long as I keep busy. You are so darn cute." She pinches Granger's cheeks. "I have your favorite flavor in stock. I put it in the back just for you."

He licks his lips as if he can taste bright blueberry ice cream. "Can I go get it," he asks, tugging her hand.

"I'll help the customers if you want to take him." I pull an apron off the hook, tying it around my waist. I lay my wallet and phone on the ledge under the counter.

They skate off, with Granger skipping in front of her. I serve up waffle cones with double scoops of chocolate ice cream and ring them up before they come back. "Your after-school rush must be over," I say, watching the door close behind the last customer.

"It won't be busy again until after dinnertime," she says, carrying a carton of ice cream to put in the cold display.

"Dang it!" Granger growls when he licks his cone, and a blue blob of ice cream falls to the tile floor.

"It's alright." I reach for the roll of paper towels. "Clean it up, and I'll buy you another one."

He gets on his hands and knees and starts wiping it up. Sunlight beams through the door when it opens, and the man that was sitting in his car watching the kids on the playground comes inside. An instant chill runs up my spine. Out of instinct, I nudge Granger with my knee and place my finger to my lips, telling him to stay quiet.

The man jerks the door closed and turns the lock.

"What can I help you with," Etta Mae asks with a deep crevice between her brows.

When he turns to face us, he's holding a large hunting knife. Etta Mae gasps and falters back.

He saunters to the counter, dragging his dirty hand across it.

Etta opens the register and takes out the cash. "Take this and leave," she says.

"I don't think he's here for the money," I say softly. "Are you following me?" I ask, keeping Granger between me and the counter. I feel his little hand wrap around my leg.

"You're Methany's girl," he says, with a deep scratch in his tone. "Where's the kid? I saw you come in with him."

"River picked him up," I respond, not taking my eyes off him.

"I didn't see him leave," he says, glaring at me and lifting the knife in my direction.

"Please, we don't want any trouble," Etta Mae says with her lip trembling.

"He took his son and left out the back door," I tell him.

"You." He points the knife at Etta Mae. "Come here." She moves from behind the counter, and he snatches her hand. "Show me the back," he growls, then looks over his shoulder. "If you try to leave, I'll kill her."

When his back is turned, I have Granger crawl to the small pantry behind the counter covered by a red-purple curtain and hand him my phone. "Find your uncle Chase's number but don't say a word. Just let him listen," I tell him. "And whatever you do, don't come out."

I hurriedly stand where he left me.

He returns with Etta Mae, who has tears filling her eyes, and shoves her toward me. I clasp her shaking hand in mine. He glances behind the counter.

The scar on his chin is deeper than I remember, and he has a look of evil in his eyes. "You were at the school looking for his son, weren't you?" I ask with a painful knot in my stomach, and the sight of him this close makes my back tingle.

"He's misinformed you. The boy is my son!" he snarls, slamming his empty hand on the counter. "Where the hell is the boy!" he screams with spit flying from his mouth.

Fear must taste like that sharp flavor at the back of my throat. His question swoops down on me like an angry swallow coveting a barn. "I told you, he left with his father." I keep my voice from wavering.

He takes a step toward Etta, and I move in front of her to keep him away from her.

"Methany stole him from me, and I plan on making him pay," he sneers.

My pulse pounds in my throat with fear like I've never felt, even amid the danger with my father. "I'm telling you, the boy isn't here. Please just leave."

He lifts the knife and smashes the handle with the glass breaker into the ice cream case, shattering the glass. "You're lying to me!" he seethes.

His gaze rolling over me gives me the creeps. I raise my hands. "If it's me you want, let her go," I say, indicating Etta Mae with a tilt of my head.

"So she can run to the cops. I don't think so." His chuckle is as ugly as his sneer.

He walks around to the other side of the counter, dragging the tip of the knife on the wood as the broken glass crunches beneath his shoes. "That ring on your finger tells me you and River are more than just friends."

"What does that have to do with anything?" My voice cracks.

"The boy is of no actual interest to me. It's Methany I want to hurt. You'll be the perfect way to do that."

"I don't know what your problem is with him, but I'm sure if you'd talk to him, the two of you could work things out."

"If I wanted to deal with him directly, I'd have gone to his place." He spins on his heel, facing me. "You all looked so happy at dinner the other night. I couldn't help but follow him home."

"You were at the restaurant?" My brows draw deep.

"Imagine how I must have felt seeing you all laughing and toasting around the table while I've been in agony. He had me thrown in prison for something he was responsible for." He leans on the counter. "Did he tell you it's because of him I had to kill my wife?"

"You're Darrell, right?" I stare at him.

"That would be me. So you have heard of me." He raps his knuckles on the wood, and I flinch.

"You beat your wife to death. How does that make it River's fault?" I ask with an even tone, so he doesn't think I'm terrified, which I am.

"You ever been cheated on?" He sneers at me. "Of course not. Why would any man in his right mind cheat on a woman that looks like you?" he scoffs.

"As a matter of fact, my ex-husband cheated on me several times." I stand tall.

"Then you know how it feels. It makes a man do crazy things." He taps his index finger to his temple. "I bet you had thoughts of killing your spouse."

"It never crossed my mind." What's he talking about? River would never sleep with another man's wife. My heart aches, knowing Granger must listen to any of this about his father.

"Jealousy is an evil bitch. Methany took something from me he can never repay. I've been rotting in a jail cell while he goes on with his life like nothing happened. He claimed to be so in love with my wife, and then as soon as he's cleared, he hotfoots it out of town, leaving her memory behind, along with what should've been rightly mine."

"I'm not sure what you're talking about," I say softly.

"When I find the boy, I'll do what he did to me. It will be the one thing that guts him."

"Please, I can't help you. His son was picked up already. I'm sure he's home by now."

"Oh, you can help me, alright." He walks over to the door, peering out between the colors of the paint. "When he finds out I'm holding you hostage, he'll show his face." He turns back around. "You think I'm a madman? Sweetheart, you ain't even begun to see my wrath." He reaches over the counter, tucking a lock of my hair behind my ear. It's everything I can do not to strike out. "Don't touch me!" I yell.

"Don't you hurt her!" Granger screams, pushing back the curtain. I grab him by the arm before he can bolt at Darrell. I shove him behind me.

"You're as much of a liar as Methany!" he rages.

Etta Mae pushes down her fear, locking arms with me, hiding Granger behind us like a solid wall.

CHAPTER TWENTY TWO

RIVER

"Drive them to the river," I yell, riding hard alongside our ranch hands, moving the cattle.

Walker, who the last time I saw, was breaking a horse, rides toward me at a fast trot. "River!" he hollers, with one hand beside his mouth, the other gripping the saddle.

I veer my horse in his direction, slowing in front of him. "What's wrong?" I know in my gut something has happened.

"You need to come back with me now. Chase has been trying to reach you."

I never carry my phone on me when we're driving the cattle. Without asking a question, we take off in a run back to the main house, leaping off when we make it to the barn. I bolt inside the house. Knox and Mercy are pacing the kitchen around the bar top.

"What is it?" I ask, out of breath.

Mercy snatches my phone from the counter, holding it out. "Chase is waiting for your call."

I bite my lip, wanting to yell just tell me, but it must be bad if they're throwing it all back on him. "What happened?" I bark into the phone when he answers.

"Darrell has Granger and Greer held hostage at the ice cream shop downtown," he says, and my heart falls to the floor. "My men and I have the entire block covered, and we're assessing the situation. Evidently, he's been watching them. Greer called the principal earlier in the day with a complaint about a man she had seen previously on the campus, watching them on the playground today."

"Why the hell didn't she call you?" I snap, grabbing the keys to my truck.

"She wouldn't have known what Darrell looked like, and you never told her he was a possible threat," he responds.

"This is all my fault. I should've listened to you." I gulp back hysteria. "You have to get in there and get them out before he kills them." I slam my truck door and start the motor as Walker and Blaise climb inside, carrying their shotguns.

Mercy and Knox both come marching out the door. "We're coming with you," Knox hollers.

"No, you're not. I don't want either of you in danger," I growl.

"You can either take us with you, or we're driving ourselves, but there is no way in Hades we're sitting around here waiting to hear what happens," Mercy barks.

"Fine." I grit my teeth. "Get in."

I drive like a maniac over the ruts in the road, flying through town until I screech to a halt three blocks from the ice cream shop due to the road blockade Chase has set up. The streets are filled with police cars. Chase is in the middle, bellowing orders. I push my way through them.

"Tell me what's happening?" I demand.

"What we've learned is that Darrell fled town almost as soon as they released him from jail. He never checked in with his probation officer. According to one lady that works in the front office at the school, last week Greer had told her about a parent that was lost in an area he shouldn't have been. We believe it was Darrell."

"So he followed her once she left the campus.

How the hell did you find out he's holding them captive?"

His hand lands on my arm, and he pulls me aside. "I got a call from Greer's cell phone. It was on speaker, and I could hear Darrell talking in the background. I traced her phone."

Mercy gasps behind me. "I was supposed to pick him up from school today, but I asked Greer if she could bring him home. If I would've picked him up, he wouldn't be in there," she sobs.

"What was he saying?" My voice is strained as I reach for Mercy's hand, trying to console her.

"You're his target. He told her you stole something from him, and he wants his revenge?"

"Stole something? I don't know what in the hell he's talking about. He took Paige from me!"

Chase stares at his feet. "There's more."

"Tell me, damn it!"

"From what I can gather from the conversation, he didn't know Granger was in the shop. Greer must have hidden him."

"That's good," I say.

"Until..."

"Until what!" My anger is getting the better of me.

"When Darrell threatened Greer, Granger

screamed at him. That's when the phone went dead."

My world spins, and I feel woozy. I apply pressure to my temples to steady myself. "We have to get them out of there."

"I've got a sniper trying to get an advantage point, but the only visual is through the glass door, and it's distorted with the painting of the ice cream cone on it."

"I'll get a vantage point," Walker grumbles, storming off with his rifle in his hand.

"I think our best and safest bet is for you to call Greer's phone. He'll see your name flashing on it and will pick it up."

I go back to my truck and snatch my phone off the seat, and lean on the open door with one hand as I call her. It rings three times before it's answered.

"I knew you'd show up eventually." Darrell laughs.

"Let them go. It's me you want. I'll come to you."

"I'll consider releasing them when you send the cops away and are standing in front of me."

"Give me ten minutes to get them cleared out, and I'll call you back. In the meantime, don't lay one finger on either of them." My voice thunders through the phone.

"The clock is ticking, pretty boy," he snips.

I hang up and turn to face Chase. "You have to get your men out of here."

"I can't do that." He shakes his head.

"You don't have a choice. He won't let me in until they're gone."

He gnaws on the inside of his cheek. "I'll get rid of them. Blaise and Walker are good shots. If you can get him in front of the door, one of them can take him out, or I will myself."

"You need to leave too," I say.

"That's not going to happen. I'll put on plain clothes and get out of sight, but I'm not leaving my nephew while Darrell terrorizes him." He calls the men together, ordering them to leave. They aren't happy about it, but they comply.

"I'll park my cruiser out of eyeshot and sneak around the back. I'll give Walker and Blaise a radio so we can communicate our locations and sight with one another." He removes his vest. "Take off your shirt and put this underneath it." He hands me the heavy black vest.

I peel out of my shirt and fasten it, then he hands me a gun. "No. If he sees it, he'll kill them." I shake him off.

"Be careful. I don't know if he's carrying a gun or

not. I'm assuming he has some sort of weapon he's threatening them with.

I call Darrell as I walk toward the building. "The police are gone. I'm headed inside. Send my son and Greer out."

"You aren't giving the orders. I am. I'll free them when I'm damn good and ready," he growls.

Sweat pours down my forehead when I walk down the block. I steady my hand as I open the glass doors to the ice cream shop. I'm grateful it's not the halls of the school I'm walking down so that no one else is in harm's way.

My boots hit hard on the tile floor, and I inhale sharply several times, standing just inside the doorway.

Darrell has a knife pressed against Greer's throat, and Granger is behind her, clinging to her leg. "Daddy!" he cries as Etta Mae tries to pull him off.

"It's going to be okay, Son," I say, holding my hand up.

"It's the man of the hour," Darrell sneers, clicking his tongue.

"I'm here. You can let them go." My voice is calm and even, unlike the fear I'm feeling inside.

"I think I want your fiancée to hear what I have to say."

"The boy and Etta don't need to be part of this." I take one step inside the store.

He tilts his head to look at Granger. "Go!" he yells. "You too," he tells Etta.

Granger gazes up at Greer before he runs to me. "I don't want to leave Mommy," he cries.

"Mommy. How sweet." Darrell's laugh is laced with anger.

"I'm not going to leave her. Aunt Mercy is outside waiting for you. I want you to go to her and stay put. Daddy and Greer will be fine."

He peers over his shoulder at Greer. "I love you," he sniffs.

"I love you, too, little man. You were so brave."

"That's enough bullshit. Get the hell out of here before I change my mind." Darrell waves the knife around.

"Go, and don't look back," I tell him, ushering him out of the door along with Etta, and he runs. I don't take my eyes off him until he's down the block in Mercy's arms.

"Come in and take a seat," Darrell orders.

I ease into a chair so as not to spook him while I assess my surroundings. The door is to the back left of me. When he turns, I see another knife tucked beneath his belt. Assessing the surroundings for anything that could be used as a weapon, there's a heavy glass water pitcher by the oversized sink. Greer's gaze connects with mine, and she seems to have read my thoughts.

"I've waited years for this moment." He loosens his grip slightly on the knife but keeps it near her skin.

"What? To terrorize your son? Didn't you do enough harm to him, beating his mother in front of him and leaving her to die?"

"My son, you say." He chuckles. "I have a secret. You're the reason I had to kill her."

"Why? Because I loved her?"

"Do you recall when Granger was born prematurely?"

"Yes. What does that have to do with anything?" My brows furrow.

"I had the doctor run his DNA."

"So," I snap.

"Turns out, he's not my son. His blood type didn't match mine, so that left you," he seethes, his spit flying out.

"That can't be." I breathe out.

"My little wifey told me about the day before we ran off and got hitched. She got on her knees and begged me to forgive her for running to you for comfort."

Visions flutter through my head. Paige called me, crying. She caught Darrell in a lie and ended things with him. She asked me to come over. Like a heart-sick puppy dog, I went as fast as my feet would take me. She promised she was done with him and would never take him back. She cried in my arms for hours, then she kissed me. I was too weak to resist her. She'd been all I'd ever wanted since the first time we'd made love. The only thing that was going through my mind was that I loved her, and this was my chance to prove it to her. I didn't use a condom, but she swore she was on the pill. I never questioned her about the day Granger was born. She wouldn't keep such a secret from me. The next day, she texted me, telling me she was sorry, but she loved Darrell and was running off to marry him. It was the second to last time she broke my heart. The last time was the day she died.

"You're lying. Paige would've told me," I snarl.

"Here's the thing. I never shared the information with her, and I paid the doctor to shred the evidence. So, not only did you try to steal my wife from me, you took the son that should've been mine."

"It can't be," I whisper in disbelief. Granger is my son?

Greer boldly spins out of his grasp. "You didn't want either of them anyway, so why punish River for your actions?"

"I like her," he says with a disgusting smile. "She's got balls. Something Paige never had."

"You've come for revenge on me. Let her go."

He snatches her by the hair, wrapping his arm around her neck with the knife pressed into her side. "She could be my revenge. You slept with Paige. I could return the favor." He sticks out his tongue, licking the side of Greer's face.

In one move, Greer reaches out, grabs the pitcher, and smashes it into the side of his head. I leap over the counter, jump on him and knock him backward. The knife flies out of his hand under the soda machine. Clutching him by the shirt, I push him away from her. His fist slams into my jaw, but I refuse to let go of the grip I have on him. Pushing him backward, I move him from behind the counter, trading a few blows with him before shoving him against the door, pinning him for a minute, then duck out of the way. The glass shatters, and Darrell's body jerks. He looks down with his eyes wide at his chest as blood pools in a round spot on his shirt. He stumbles, hitting the counter and falling to the floor, with a loud crack to his head as it bounces off the floor. I stare at him for a few moments, then bend down, feeling for a pulse.

Greer grips my shoulder. "Is he dead?"

I nod, standing, sweeping her into my arms. "Did he hurt you?"

"No." She chokes on her emotions.

"I'm so sorry." I hold her face.

"It's not your fault."

"I found out a few days ago he had gotten out of prison. I should've told you."

"You had no idea he'd show up here. I saw him last week and didn't know who he was."

"Chase said you protected Granger. I don't know how you did it, but thank you."

"There was no way I was going to let him harm our son!" she growls.

"I know, I know," I try to soothe her.

She steps back. "Do you think he was telling the truth about Granger being your son?"

We jump when Chase, Walker, and Blaise yank open the shattered door. "Did I shoot you?" Walker is out of breath. "I took the shot when I had it. It scared me to death that bullet would go right through him into you."

"You made a clean hit. He's dead." Walker sighs in relief and draws me into his chest. "I'm alright." I can feel his heart pounding against his chest.

Chase gets on his radio, calling for an ambulance and his men to return.

"I need to see my son." I stomp out of the store and down the block.

Greer tries to follow me, but Chase stops her. "I need you to stay here and tell me exactly what happened."

CHAPTER TWENTY THREE
RIVER

"Daddy!" Granger cries as soon as he sees me. He flees from Mercy's grasp, racing into my arms.

"It's over," I say, crushing him in a hug.

"Where's Mommy?" he sobs, peering over my shoulder.

"She's inside still with Uncle Chase. He needs to ask her questions about what happened."

"That wicked man wanted to kill me," he wails. "My ice cream fell on the floor. I got on my hand and knees to clean it up, and I heard him come in being mean. Mommy told me to be quiet, and when he wasn't looking, she hid me behind a curtain so he couldn't see me. I sat so still and quiet until he said bad things about you and tried to hurt Mommy."

"You did good, Son." I hold the back of his head, pressing my lips to his forehead. "You're a brave young man. He's gone and can never harm you."

He lifts his head and places his hands on my chest, leaning back to look at me. "Is that the same man that killed my mommy?" His lip trembles.

I nod.

"He's my real daddy?" Tear pool in his eyes.

"I'm your dad, and that's all that matters," I say as I carry him to my truck. "I'm taking you to the hospital to get checked out."

"I'm not hurt," he protests.

"I want a doctor to reassure me." I buckle him.

"I can take him," Knox offers.

"No. I'll be the one at his side," I say harshly. "Get Chase to bring all of you back to the ranch." I climb inside.

"What about Greer?" Mercy asks.

"Tell her I'm sorry. I need to do this on my own."

They share a perplexed look between them, not having any idea about what Darrell alluded to about Granger.

"Ask Greer," I say, driving off.

"Are you mad at me?" Granger whimpers.

I take my eyes off the road. "Why would I be angry with you?"

"Because I've been nothing but trouble for you. I have nightmares that keep you up at night. You moved a bazillion miles away from Grandma and Grandpa, and that man wanted to kill you all because of me." He holds up one finger at a time as he makes his point.

"None of this is your fault. I know you don't understand this, but I fell in love with the wrong woman, but because of you, it ended up being the best thing that ever happened to me. I'd give up everything for you and never blink an eye. That man is sick in the head. There is no one to blame but him."

"Is Greer the wrong woman too?" He blinks his eyes several times. It's not lost on me that one minute he was calling her mommy, and he's switched to Greer because he's uncertain.

"No. She's the woman I was meant to love. She's the moon and stars to me."

He sits up and wipes his nose with his hand. "Like your tattoo."

"Yes, just like my tattoo."

I park in the emergency room lot and walk Granger inside, checking in with the receptionist. The place is empty, so the wait isn't long. They tuck us into a room close to the nurses' station. I turn on the television and hand Granger the remote. "Daddy's going to step just outside the door and speak with the nurse."

He nods, already finding a show to watch.

I step out and ask to speak to the doctor that will be examining my son. A short, older man in a white jacket comes from the back, shaking my hand.

"I got a call from Sheriff Calhoun telling me you'd be heading this way with your son. He updated me on the situation. I'll gladly check the boy out. One thing I'd highly recommend in these types of situations is therapy."

"He already sees a psychologist from previous trauma. I'll be sure to get him in right away. The thing is, he's not physically harmed, but the man that held him hostage was supposedly the boy's real father. It's a long story about how I legally adopted him. What I need from you is a DNA test. He made some bold accusations, and I need to confirm whether or not he's my son." I peer over my shoulder to make sure Granger didn't hear me. He's lost in his show, laughing as if he wasn't just traumatized.

"I see," he says. "I'll need a blood sample from both of you and his mother."

"His mother is dead."

"Alright. I'll examine him and have the nurse

draw his blood. You can sit over there." He points. "I'll request a sample of yours to be drawn out of his sight."

"Thank you. How long will it take to get the results back?"

"A couple of days. I can type his blood to see if it matches yours, but it won't be the definite answer that you're looking for."

"I understand. I'll wait for the DNA results."

The nurse takes my blood and puts a bandage on the crevice of my arm. When I walk into Granger's room, the nurse is setting up the supplies she needs to take his blood.

"I don't want you to stab me!" he squeals.

"It's alright, buddy. Look, they drew my blood too. It didn't hurt too much." I show him the bandage.

"Why did they take your blood? Did you get hurt?" Fear widens his eyes.

"No." I sit on the side of the bed, avoiding answering him. "You need to sit real still," I tell him.

"Ouch!" he yells, scrunching his nose when the needle goes into the vein.

"You're a tough guy. I've seen you get thrown from a horse and hop right back on. That little old needle ain't anything to a boy like you."

He grins. "I am strong."

"You're the toughest kid I know."

I hear Chase's voice as he's coming down the hallway. He stops in the doorway with Greer, who looks a mess.

"Is he alright?" she gulps.

"Come here." I tap the spot next to me on the bed.

She shuffles her feet and falls next to me, wrapping her arms around my neck. "I was so scared." She swallows back sobs. "I thought he was going to kill you."

"We're all going to be okay now. He's gone, and your father's in jail."

She lets go of me, clinging to Granger. "I was terrified when you came out from behind the curtain."

"I couldn't let him talk about you and my daddy," he blubbers.

"You should've stayed put," I tell him, running my hand over the top of his head.

She sniffs and sits, laying her hand on my arm. Her gaze is anchored on where my blood was drawn. "You'll know for sure," she whispers.

"It doesn't change how I feel," I rasp, getting up. I take her hand, and we walk into the hallway. "I just need to know if he was telling the truth or not. Regardless of the outcome, he's my boy, always has been."

The doctor interrupts us. "You can take your son home, Mr. Methany. He's not even got a scratch on him physically. Remember what I suggested for him," he says.

"I'll call for an appointment first thing in the morning." I shake his hand.

"I'll have the results emailed to you," he says.

"Thank you." I wrap my arm around Greer's waist. "Let's go home."

Exhaustion takes over Granger, and he falls sound asleep on the short ride home. Carrying him inside the house, Mercy rubs his back before I take him to his room, tucking him into bed. I walk back down to the living room, where everyone has gathered.

"I can't thank you all enough for what you did for me today. I know taking a man's life is never easy," I speak directly to Walker.

He nods with his jaw clenched.

"What happened in the ice cream shop?" Knox asks.

"There is no doubt in my mind that Greer saved our boy." She walks over to me, draping her arms around my waist from the side. "There's no telling what would've happened"—I swallow—"if he was still alive." I choke and, for the first time, let my tears rain down. "Darrell said he killed Paige because Granger is my son, not his." All their gazes meet back and forth at one another in disbelief.

"Paige would've told you," Mercy says and then covers her mouth with her hand.

"He claims she didn't know. He had a DNA test done when Granger was born and kept the results from her."

"The two of you were done when Darrell came into the picture." Knox frowns.

"The day before they ran off and got married, she called me, telling me they were finished. She asked me to come over, and I did." I hang my head in shame. "I'm not the cheating kind. I believed her when she said they were through. I never suspected he was mine because she insisted she was on the pill."

"Could that woman hurt you any more?" Blaise rages. "I remember picking up the pieces with you several times, and now this!"

"It's okay. This will not break me. I refuse to be angry with her any longer. What I felt for her was a childhood crush. Greer has made me see the difference. I'll always be thankful for Paige giving me a son."

"When do you get the test results back?" Chase chimes in.

"The doc said it would take about two weeks. None of it really matters, other than I wasn't there from the very beginning. I missed his first steps and his first words. But I'm the one who's been here taking care of him with the help of my family. It will be a relief if he's my biological son and he's not related to Darrell. It may help Granger heal in the process, knowing I'm his real father."

They all get up and hug me and Greer one by one.

"He's lucky to have both of you," Walker tells her.

"I'm the one who's fortunate." She smiles, and her face lights up.

We walk hand in hand to our bedroom and peel out of our clothes, getting into bed. "Would it be okay if I just hold you tonight?" Her head is already lying in the middle of my bare chest. "I'm exhausted."

"I'll hold you as long as you need."

I roll to my side, forcing her to face me. "What you did today was remarkable. I should be the one holding you." She cuddles into me, and I lay my arms protectively around her. "Our life will be better from here on out. I promise. Both of our pasts have collided, and we've survived. We deserve a happily ever after."

"I thought you didn't believe in fairy tales?"

"With you at my side, anything is possible."

CHAPTER TWENTY FOUR
RIVER

"I'm thrilled the two of you decided to get married in Salt Lick." My mother embraces Greer in a genuine hug. "I was only sorry to hear that your mother couldn't make it, dear."

"She just came home from the hospital with pneumonia. I told her we could postpone it, but she insisted on us not changing the date." My father steps in to greet her too.

"What am I? Chopped liver?" I chuckle, embracing my mother.

"Nonsense. You know you're my favorite son." She teasingly slaps me in the chest.

"Come on, Grandpa. I want to see where they are getting married." Granger tugs him away.

"Ellie, Jane, Margret, Nita, and I worked on decorating the barn and baking lots of goodies all night long. The menfolk gave the old red barn a fresh coat of paint."

"You guys didn't have to go to all that trouble. It was fine the way it was and we could've had the food catered," I tell her. "We just wanted to share the day with all of you, not make you work hard."

"We wouldn't have it any other way." Aunt Ellie holds out her arms. She spent the first ten minutes hugging Knox as if she ain't seen her in forever. "Thank you."

My mom wraps her arm inside of Greer's, and they walk a few steps in front of me, going onto the porch of the main house. "My son told me about your father and what you did with all his money. What's going to happen to all the land and his house?"

"It's all been paid off for many years. River helped get this year's cattle sold last week, so it will pay for all the ranch hands to continue to work until my father releases it to one of us to sell."

"I'm sorry about what happened to you. Not only with your family but with Darrell too. River said you saved our grandson's life."

Granger peeks over her shoulder at me. "He's a

bit dramatic with the details. I did what anyone else would've done in my situation."

"And she unscores what she did." I laugh.

"We're grateful to you and so excited about the two of you getting married."

Greer stops walking and holds her hand up with her palm facing down. "I can't tell you what it meant to me for you to give River your mother's wedding set. I'll cherish it forever."

My mom lays her hand on Greer's cheek. "I couldn't have picked a better woman for my son than you. From this day forward, you'll always be a part of this family."

"Now, don't go scaring her off," Jane says, holding open the screen door. "The Calhouns have quite a reputation in these parts." She grins.

When we enter the house, every Calhoun is inside, including my sister Rose. Mom positions Greer in the middle of all of them, introducing her to everyone she didn't meet the last time she was here.

While she's preoccupied, I check my email messages. I've been on pins and needles waiting for the DNA test results. My heart nearly stops when I see the email heading with the name of the lab they processed it through. "Excuse me," I say, stepping outside.

My finger hovers over the email as I think about the past two weeks. Granger's therapist said he was doing remarkably well with everything he's been through. In one of his sessions, all he could talk about was Greer being his mommy and that she protected him from the bad man, and that's what mommies are supposed to do. Surprisingly, he's not had the first nightmare since the incident. I woke up in the middle of the night a couple of days afterward, and Greer wasn't in bed. It scared me, thinking I'd slept through him screaming. My feet hit the floor fast and hard to his room to find her curled up on the carpet by this bed, watching him. When I asked her if he'd had a nightmare, she simply said no, but she wanted to be there if he did. My heart swelled with love for even more. She honestly loves him as her own.

I turn in a circle twice, trying to decide if this is the right time to find out. "It won't change anything. Why am I so nervous?"

"What's going on?" The screen door creaks when Greer opens it, easing onto the porch with me.

"It's the email from the lab with the DNA test results." I show her.

"Are you going to open it?" Her hand caresses my arm.

"Perhaps I should wait until we get back home."

"I think this is the perfect time and place for you to find out if he's your biological son. Your family would be so excited."

"But what if he's not?"

"Then he's not. That doesn't make him any less yours. Has your family, for even one day of his life, not loved him like they do all the others?"

"No."

"Then what are you afraid of?"

I lean down with a soft kiss on her lips. "You're right."

"I enjoy hearing that." She smiles and wipes her thumb over my lip. "Open it."

I grip the phone in my left hand and tap the email. Skipping over the introduction part, I scan the results. "He's mine," I whisper at first. Then I pick her up in my arms, swinging her around. "He's mine!" I yell at the top of my lungs, then kiss her hard. "He's ours," I say, locking my gaze with hers.

"He always was," she simply states.

"What's all the hollering about?" My mother comes running out.

"I'll tell you, but I need to speak with Granger first."

"He's still out at the barn with his grandpa." She points.

I kiss Greer one more time. "I need to do this alone. Are you okay with that?"

"Perfectly. Go tell your son."

I jump off the stairs into a full sprint to the barn. I'm taken aback when I see what they've done to the place. White lights twinkle from the ceiling, and there are canna lilies everywhere. It's the first time I recall the place not smelling like a horse's behind. Granger is chatting away with my father about how much he loves his calf, and he wants him to meet him.

"Hey," I say, tapping him on the shoulder. "I need to steal you away from Grandpa for a few minutes."

"Everything okay?" My dad's thick dark brow furrows.

"Perhaps you should hear this when he does. You've always understood how I've loved this little guy as my very own. Grandpa Chet felt the same way about you, and Momma did the same for my sister."

"What are you getting at?" he asks.

I squat on Granger's level. "When the dangerous

man held you and Greer hostage, he said some things I needed to know if they were true or not."

"What sort of things?" He scrunches his nose.

"Remember when I made you go to the hospital to get checked out, and they drew blood?"

He rubs his elbow as if he is being stuck. "It hurt."

"It did. I'm sorry, but I needed them to run a test for me."

His eyes grow wide. "Am I sick?"

"No, Son, you're not." I chuckle. "I had mine done too."

"What did the results say?" I get the feeling my dad knows where this is leading.

"All these years, we thought the bad man was your father. He's not." I keep my gaze on him to gauge his reaction.

"Then who is?" His little brows fold in the middle.

"I am, and this test proves it. You're my flesh and blood."

"Really?" he squeals, throwing his arms around me.

"Not that I haven't thought of you as my own since you were three, but yes, really."

Dad's large, weathered hand rests on my shoulder. I look up to see a single tear slide down his face. My father never cries. "I love you, son," he says in his deep, gruff voice filled with emotion.

I hike Granger on my hip and stand, hugging my father. "I love you, too, Dad."

"Does this mean Greer is my real mommy?" Granger asks me with his hands on either side of my face. "Paige was your birth mother, but Greer will be your forever mommy."

"Yay!" He fists-bumps the air.

"I need to go inside and tell everyone else."

"I want to tell them." Granger fights to get out of my arms and runs as fast as he can to the main house with my dad behind us.

"Guess what, everybody?" he hollers with more excitement than I've ever seen from him. "Daddy is my daddy!"

They all look confused. "What he means is that he and I have the same DNA," I clear my throat to clarify.

"That's the best news ever," my mom says, crying when Granger climbs in her lap.

Everyone takes the time to congratulate me, and Aunt Nita brings out a bottle of champagne to celebrate. "Let's toast to the good news and the wedding that will take place here tomorrow morning."

After things settle down, the women scoop Greer off to have girl time. I've heard stories of my family's girl time, so I'm sure they are going to indoctrinate her into the Calhoun ways. I should be afraid, but it makes my heart feel good knowing how much they adore her.

Uncle Bear built a bonfire and has a cooler full of ice-cold beer waiting on us to join him. The grill is full of hot dogs and hamburgers, with a side of crispy pork belly. "I know this is your favorite," he says, handing me a piece.

"I do miss this. I miss all of you."

"We feel the same, but we're happy things are finally working out for you. I hear you run a damn good cattle ranch," Uncle Ethan states, coming up behind me.

"Thanks to you, I got top dollar this year."

"I just spread the word about how good your cattle was. You did the rest. It really impressed my buddy with the way you handled yourself."

"I had a few excellent teachers." I laugh.

We spend the rest of the evening reminiscing about old times. All of my cousins are here. Chase, Walker, Blaise, Mercy, and Knox all made the trip with us. It's good to have everyone in one place. These are rare moments, and I'll cherish them.

A yawn escapes along with a hard stretch right about midnight. "I'm getting old," I snort. "It's way past my bedtime, and tomorrow's going to be a busy day." I stand, patting Uncle Ian on the back.

"I'll see to it the fire gets put out." He grabs a hose.

"Good night, son." My dad hugs me for a long time before he releases me. "I'm proud of the choices you've made."

"Thanks, Dad. That means a lot to me."

"I'll walk you back to our house in case you've forgotten the way," he teases.

We make the trek on the familiar dirt path, and the porch light is on like always. My mother would never turn it off unless everyone was home where they belonged. Her words, not mine.

She and Greer are sitting on the couch, looking as if they've been up to no good and a little tipsy.

She stumbles into my arms. "Did you have a good time?" I laugh, smelling the liquor on her breath.

"Your momma and aunts have dirty minds." She thinks she's whispering, but she's loud.

"Now you've seen what I've dealt with all these years," my dad snorts, helping mom off the couch.

"You love when I talk dirty," she slurs.

"I'm taking your mother to bed," he says, clutching her around the waist.

"Now we're talking." She squeezes his ass.

"I'm so sorry you had to see that," I howl.

"Are you taking me to bed, cowboy?" she asks, then her head falls on my shoulder. I snicker and bend down, placing my arms behind her knees, picking her up, and carrying her to bed.

CHAPTER TWENTY FIVE
RIVER

"Where is your bride-to-be this morning?" Mom is taking a pan of homemade biscuits out of the oven, and my stomach growls at the heavenly smell.

"She's still sleeping. I think she might be a little hungover this morning."

"Don't you worry, I have the fix for that. She'll be perfectly fine by the time she walks down the aisle." She plates the biscuits and sets them in the middle of the table.

"Sounds like you ladies had fun last night. I hope you didn't corrupt my soon-to-be wife." I sit, grabbing a hot biscuit. "These are my favorite." I bounce it from hand to hand.

"Why do you think I got up at the butt crack of dawn to make them?" She points the spatula at me.

"Because you love me." I give her a cheesy grin like I did when I was a kid. "Where's Granger?"

"He spent the night at the main house with Rose and Missy."

"I'm sure they spoiled him rotten. He'll never want to come home with me."

"He's looking forward to Greer being his momma. He'll go home just fine." She sits across from me, wiping her hands on her apron. "Are you ready for today?"

"I can hardly wait," I answer without hesitation.

"There was a time I didn't think this day would ever get here for you. I was so distraught with worry when you had your heart broken over Paige."

"I'm good now, Mom." I reach across, holding her hand. "You don't have to fret anymore."

"Good."

"What time is it?" Greer comes out of the bedroom in one of my long T-shirts, rubbing her eyes with her fists.

"It's time for you not to be seen by the groom." Mom stands, ushering her back into the bedroom. "Grab you a plate of biscuits and move along. Your tux is in the main house. Noah and Molly have been taking care of it."

The front door opens, and Uncle Wyatt and Aunt Margret stroll inside. "It's time for you to come with me," Uncle Wyatt says.

"Your bride will be in excellent hands." Aunt Margret pinches my cheeks like she used to when I was a young boy.

"Please don't scare off Greer." I wag my finger.

"Honey, if she didn't run for the hills last night, she ain't ever leaving," she hoots.

"I think the older you ladies get, the naughtier you are." I crack up.

"That's the way it should be." Uncle Wyatt laughs. "You'll learn to appreciate their sense of humor. Come on, boy."

"I'll always be a boy to you, won't I?" I follow him out.

"It's a term of endearment. I think you've become a man all of us are proud of." He slaps me on the back.

Mercy, Knox, Aunt Jane, and Aunt Molly are already drinking mimosas at the kitchen table, giggling.

"Wait until you see what my mother got Greer

for a wedding night gift." Knox snorts so hard her drink comes out of her nose.

"Please don't tell me," I scoff.

"You'll find out soon enough." Aunt Jane raises her glass. "And you'll thank me in the morning," she howls.

Uncle Ethan shakes his head, looking down. "I should've warned you," he mumbles.

"It's alright. You forget I was raised by the queen of dirty minds."

"Uh-uh, you gotta get upstairs and get dressed." Molly hops up. "And so do we."

"We don't want to keep the bride waiting." Mercy and Knox tip their glasses one more time.

"Your tux is in Blaise's old room," Uncle Noah states.

"Thanks." I march up the stairs and open his bedroom door. It hasn't changed one bit. I've had many sleepovers in this room and gotten into tons of trouble. The tux is hanging in a bag in the closet. My mother called me a week or so ago and got all my measurements so she could order the right size. I'd prefer to get married in a pair of blue jeans and cowboy boots, but she insisted just once I dress up. It made her happy, so I agreed.

She told me they had Grandma Amelia's dress

redesigned for Greer. I'm picturing some yellowed old potato sack-looking thing. It doesn't matter what she's wearing. I'd marry her stark naked and be just fine with it.

While I dress, my father and Granger come to check on me. "You look mighty handsome," I tell my son, who's wearing a navy suit with a bolo tie.

"Grandpa made me dress up." He pouts.

"Well, if it makes you feel any better, your grandmother forced me too." I chuckle.

"You both look good. Are you ready?" Dad asks, straightening my tie.

A moment of panic hits me. "Who's walking Greer down the aisle?"

"She asked me to," he says. "I told her I'd be honored."

"Thank you." I hug him.

We all walk down the stairs together, and the house is empty. They've all made their way to the barn. Uncle Ian got ordained so he could marry us. I meet him underneath the flowered altar and wait for the music to start. Uncle Bear and Missy play the wedding march on the guitar, and Greer appears at the back of the barn with her hand lying on my father's arm. Her dress is crisp white and cut off the shoulders with little shiny pearls sparingly over the lacy bottom part of the gown. The top half is silk and fits perfectly to her breasts. You'd never know her dress is vintage. They did an amazing job of redesigning it for Greer. You'd think it was made just for her. Her black hair is pulled up with strands curled around her face. She has a smidgen of makeup on her lips and cheeks. She's the prettiest thing I've ever seen. My face already hurts from smiling so much.

Granger strolls down the aisle first and sits beside my mother. When Greer makes her way to me, my dad places her hands in mine.

"You look gorgeous," I whisper.

"And you look mighty handsome in a tux, cowboy." The corner of her lips quirks upward as her gaze scrolls my body with an appreciative look.

Uncle Ian does the typical ceremony with a few laughs in between. "Do you have the ring?" he asks Granger, who fumbles with it, handing it to me. "I understand you've written your own vows."

Greer's brows pop up with excitement. "I can't wait to hear yours."

Everyone laughs.

"You first," Uncle Ian tells her.

She takes my hand, holding the black matte

band on the end of my ring finger, and gently slides it on.

"I know I told you I never wanted to marry again, but you changed that for me. I've never felt so loved, not only by you but your entire family." She glances at them, then into my eyes. "I've seen your kindness and strength. I've also seen you patient and frayed. I vow to tolerate when you're grumpy." Everyone laughs. "You are my favorite person, along with your son, who has stolen my heart as well," she says, peeking around me to smile at him. "I choose you to be my partner in life and to continue to be playful with you until we're old and decrepit." She winks at my mother. "I vow to take you as my husband, cheerfully exchanging my heart for yours."

"Your turn." Ian nudges me. "I don't think it can get any better than that," he teases.

I clear my throat, shoving down my nerves, sliding the ring on her finger. "I choose you over and over, Greer Alden, to spend the rest of my days with, loving you every moment. I realize I'm a lot of work, but I promise I'll be worth it. We have lots of roads to travel together, and I'm looking forward to every single one of them. I love you more than I ever thought possible, and I choose you to always be at my side." I hold my hand to my chest. "I'd gather the sun, the moon, and the stars..."

"For the ones I love..." she finishes my sentence and jumps into my arms, kissing me as if there is not anyone else in the barn.

SNEAK PEEK AT BOOK 3

Old Dirt Road
Whiskey River West
Book 3

CHAPTER ONE

MERCY

"How did your interview go today?"

I answer Chase's question with the slam of the door.

"That good, huh?" He takes a bottle down from a cabinet and pours a dark brown drink out of a fifth of whiskey, swirling it in the glass before he hands it to me.

I knock it back in one gulp. "The bastard lives in the middle ages. He stuck his crooked nose up at me because I'm a woman," I say through the burn of the whiskey.

"I heard through the grapevine that Stephens is a hard-ass."

"And a male chauvinist pig, to be exact." I hand him the glass for a refill.

"I guess there aren't too many female livestock agents in this neck of the woods. I could make some phone calls if you'd like. And I'm sure Uncle Ethan has some connections."

"Don't you dare. I wore Stephens down, and he agreed to an audition." I use finger quotes. "I'll show him what I'm made of, and he'll have no other choice than to hire me for the job."

"I'm sure you'll kick ass." He chuckles, putting the bottle of whiskey back on the shelf. "Granger is going to miss having you around all the time."

"I'll miss him, too, but River and Greer have a schedule worked out, so they won't need me as much." I shrug. "Besides, it will be good to have something for myself."

"I couldn't agree more. I felt the same way when I took over the interim sheriff position. Being a rancher was never my dream, but I was glad to lend a hand until this place got settled. It's running like a well-oiled machine. I'll be handing it over to the new man anytime now." He glances at his watch.

"This town is lucky to have you." I playfully swat his cheek.

"Now that Greer's father is locked away, things will settle down, and I can focus on improving things and hiring good men and women to protect this town from the Aldens of the world."

"What's the new ranch foreman like?" I sit on the counter of the breakfast bar.

"He's a tall drink of sweet iced tea," Knox says, batting her lashes as she walks into the room.

"You've met him?"

"I helped Chase interview him."

"Where was I?" I laugh.

"You were knee-deep into teaching Granger how to make spaghetti."

"If I recall, he wore more of it than he actually cooked." I squint.

"That he did," Chase huffs.

"We could use a handsome cowboy around here," I say, hopping to my feet.

"There will be no hanky-panky with the men." Chase aims a stern finger in my direction.

"Oh, come on. Mercy could use a little cobweb cleaning from the womb broom," Knox snorts.

Chase's face turns beet red. My arms cross over my chest. "You asked for that one," I snicker. "But you leave my cobwebs out of it." I wink and can't keep from grinning.

"I'm just saying, it's been like...forever." She taps her pointer finger to her chin.

"You're one to talk," I scoff.

"This is way more than I need or want to know." Chase makes an uncomfortable facial expression.

"When's the last time you did the squat thrust in the cucumber patch?" Knox howls at Chase.

He spews the whiskey that was dancing on his lips across the room. "You are out of control, and it ain't none of your damn business." His tone says he's aggravated with her, but the smile playing on his face tells another story. He wipes his mouth with the back of his hand. "All I'm saying is the two of you need to look for men elsewhere. I don't want you distracting our employees."

"Then perhaps you should hire men who fell out of the ugly tree and hit every branch on the way down." I smirk.

"There ain't enough whiskey in the house to deal with the likes of you two." He chuckles, stomping out the back door.

"I love getting a rise out of him." Knox lifts her hand for a high five to meet with mine.

"You two tormenting him?" River skips through the door that Chase exited.

"You're next." I giggle, rinsing out my glass.

"Did you get the job?" He ignores me.

"Not yet, but I will."

"You know you don't have to work outside the ranch, right? You keep things in proper working order around here. You did way more than take care of Granger."

"I know, but I really want to do this. Besides, I'm good at multitasking. I can still keep up with what I do for the ranch."

"If it gets to be too much, you'll let me know." He grasps my shoulder.

"It won't be. I promise."

"Damn, that's a sweet ride," Knox says, standing on her tiptoes and looking out the kitchen window.

"I love the oversized tires on the Jeep Gladiator. Looks totally badass." I peer over her shoulder.

"That must be the new foreman." River shuffles his boots to the door. "Chase tells me he won't be living on the property. He bought the small barn down the old dirt road before the stop sign. He's been living there the last several weeks, remodeling it, according to Chase.

"He sounds perfect for you, Knox." I nudge her arm with mine.

"Nah, I'm way too busy to pay him any mind. I've got my hands full with lumber being delivered this week to build the first house on the ranch."

"Momma always said the best things in life can

be found on an old dirt road. But what I don't understand is why he wouldn't want room and board as part of his job?"

"It was offered to him. He chose to be on his own. I can't say I blame him. Who wants to live in a house with ten other men if they don't have to?" River steps outside.

"I should build a tiny home for him on the property," Knox says, falling in behind him with me on her heels.

"Where'd this guy come from?" I ask out of curiosity.

"He was working on a ranch in Billings. Prior to that, I have no idea. Chase has all the information on him."

As we make our way in this direction, I take note that his Jeep is set up as if he could bug-out at any time. It has a tent loaded on the side that installs on top of it. Racks are on either side of the roof, and large white jugs are nestled on a platform on the tailgate. When we make it to where he and Chase are standing, they have their backs to us, shaking hands. Chase hears us and turns in our direction. My mouth gaps to the ground when the man turns around. He has to be the hottest man I've ever laid eyes on. He's sporting a tan-colored hat with a leather band on the brim. His chin is chiseled to perfection, with a neatly trimmed mustache and a dark goatee draping his face. His hazel eyes are as sexy as the rest of him. Biceps bulge from beneath his white T-shirt, screaming to be free. His chest is broad, and he narrows at the waist, with thighs tight in his well-worn jeans. I'd love to see him stark naked. He'd be something to be admired.

"This is our new ranch foreman, Hardin," Chase says, introducing him. He shakes hands with River and quickly cuts a gaze at me, then Knox, who is openly drooling.

"It's nice to have you on board," River tells him. "Chase and I will be showing you the ranch and introducing you to the men. You'll meet with Mercy later to go over costs and expenses." River angles toward me.

He nods without a word.

"Do you have a last name?" I ask.

"Just Hardin," he responds, barely looking at me.

I'll try a different approach for conversation. "Where are you from?"

"A little bit of everywhere. No place specific." He bites his bottom lip as if he's gracing me with his answers.

He's hiding something. I wonder how well Chase

vetted him for the position. Either that, or he's an arrogant jerk face. Could be that I'm already riled up from my interview this morning with a man that doesn't think I qualify for a job simply because I'm a woman. His good looks suddenly don't appeal to me anymore.

"Alright. We'll meet you back at the house once we're done," River says, and they head toward the ATVs.

"Friendly sort," I snark to Knox.

"Maybe he's just a private kinda guy."

"Or he's hiding something."

"You're always so suspicious. Give him a chance to settle down."

"I'm not interested anyway. He's totally not my type."

"Tall, dark, muscular, sexy, and a cowboy to boot." She shrugs. "What's not to like?"

"Looks aren't everything."

"They sure don't hurt none." She giggles. "Especially in the sack."

"He's all yours," I say, walking back to the house.

"Have you even looked at a guy since Taylor died..."

I stop dead in my tracks. "Taylor is an off-limit topic for me," I bark harshly.

"It's been eight years. How long you going to hold on to the guilt for something you didn't do?"

"I don't think it will ever be something I can shake off." I blink several times, fighting off tears.

"One moment in time should not define the rest of your life. You have so much love to give, and yet, you keep everyone but family at arm's length. You're always wanting to fix everyone else's problems but your own." She folds her arms over her chest and taps the toe of her boot in the grass. "Any outsider, you maintain a surface relationship to keep from getting hurt. You're missing out on love."

I stomp up the steps. "I don't want to be loved."

Knox snags my elbow. "You're twenty-six years old. Don't you ever want a family of your own?" Her voice softens.

"I have you guys, and that's all I need."

"Don't be angry with me. I love you, and I just want you to be happy. You are so hard on yourself."

"I'm perfectly happy being by myself. I will never allow that kind of pain again in my life, even if it means being alone." I feel the ache as if it were yesterday.

"Alright, I'll back off, but know that I'm here whenever you need me." She tucks a strand of my black hair behind my ear.

"I do, and thank you for caring about me." I hug her.

"You're my best friend and the only one that puts up with my antics." She giggles.

"I'm going into the office to pull reports so I can be ready to go over them with mister not-so-friend-ly," I snark.

"I'm sure once he gets to know you, he'll be all smiles and lose the coy attitude."

"Keeping things professional is all I care about."

Greer opens the door as I go to open it. "You two okay?" she asks, seeing my eyes misty.

"Yeah, nothing to worry about." I shrug it off as I walk past her into the office with her following me.

"I'm taking Granger to the ice cream shop. Do you want to tag along?"

"Do you think he's actually going to go inside this time?" She's taken him several times since the incident with Darrell, but he freezes at the door.

"I hope so. The psychiatrist says it's important that he does to help alleviate his fears."

"He seems so much better in every other aspect. The last nightmare he had was right after it happened. I feel like him knowing River is really his father has helped him more than anything, and you being a permanent part his life."

"He's a tough little boy. I'm confident we'll get through it together." She turns and walks to the door, looking over her shoulder. "By the way, did you get a chance to meet Hardin?"

I purse my lips. "I did."

"If I wasn't a married woman…" She grins.

"Not you too," I huff, clasping my hands on the desk. "I wouldn't let my cousin know you think he's hot, or he might be out of a job."

"River is the only man that will ever own my heart." She laughs. "But Hardin is sure easy on the eyes."

ABOUT THE AUTHOR

"This author has the magical ability to take an already strong and interesting plot and add so many unexpected twists and turns that it turns her books into a complete addiction for the reader." Dandelion Inspired Blog

www.kellymooreauthor.com to join newsletter and get a free book.

Armed with books in the crook of my elbow, I can go anywhere. That's my philosophy! Better yet, I'll write the books that will take me on an adventure.

My heroes are a bit broken but will make you swoon. My heroines are their own kick-ass characters armed with humor and a plethora of sarcasm.

If I'm not tucked away in my writing den, with coffee firmly gripped in hand, you can find me with a book propped on my pillow, a pit bull lying across my legs, a Lab on the floor next to me, and two kittens running amuck.

My current adventure has me living in Idaho with my own gray-bearded hero, who's put up with my shenanigans for over thirty years, and he doesn't mind all my book boyfriends.

If you love romance, suspense, military men, lots of action and adventure infused with emotion, tear-worthy moments, and laugh-out-loud humor, dive into my books and let the world fall away at your feet.

ALSO BY KELLY MOORE

Whiskey River West Series

Gathering the Sun

Moon & Stars

Old Dirt Road Fall 2022

Whiskey River Road Series - Available on Audible

Coming Home, Book 1

Stolen Hearts, Book 2

Three Words, Book 3

Kentucky Rain, Book 4

Wild Ride, Book 5

Magnolia Mill, Book 6

Rough Road, Book 7

Lucky Man, Book 8

Simple Man, Book 9

The Vineyard, Book 10

The Broken Pieces Series in order

Broken Pieces

Pieced Together

Piece by Piece

Pieces of Gray

Syn's Broken Journey

Broken Pieces Box set Books 1-3

August Series in Order

Next August

This August

Seeing Sam

The Hitman Series- Previously Taking Down
Brooklyn/The DC Seres

Stand By Me - On Audible as Deadly Cures

Stay With Me On Audible as Dangerous Captive

Hold Onto Me

Epic Love Stories Series can be read in any order

Say You Won't Let Go. Audiobook version

Fading Into Nothing Audiobook version

Life Goes On. Audiobook version

Gypsy Audiobook version

Jameson Wilde Audiobook version

Rescue Missions Series can be read in any order

Imperfect. On Audible

Blind Revenge

Fated Lives Series

Rebel's Retribution Books 1-4. Audible

Theo's Retaliation Books 5-7. Audible

Thorn's Redemption Audible

Fallon's Revenge Book 11 Audible

The Crazy Rich Davenports Season One in order of reading

The Davenports On Audible

Lucy

Yaya

Ford

Gemma

Daisy

The Wedding

Halloween Party

Bang Bang

Coffee Tea or Me

21783518R00174